D0035275

Genies, Meanies, and Magic Rings

RETOLD BY
Stephen Mitchell

Genies, Meanies, and Magic Rings

Three Tales from *The Arabian Nights*

ILLUSTRATIONS BY
Tom Pohrt

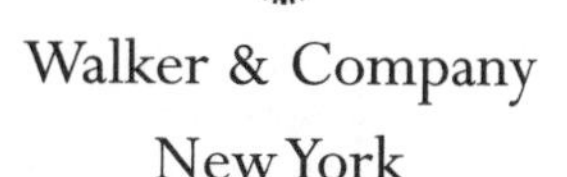

Walker & Company
New York

First published in the United States of America in 2007 by
Walker Publishing Company, Inc.
Distributed to the trade by Holtzbrinck Publishers

For information about permission to reproduce selections from
this book, write to Permissions, Walker & Company,
104 Fifth Avenue, New York, New York 10011

Library of Congress Cataloging-in-Publication Data
Mitchell, Stephen.
Genies, meanies, and magic rings : three tales from the Arabian nights /
retold by Stephen Mitchell ; illustrations by Tom Pohrt.
p. cm.
Summary: A retelling of three tales from the "Arabian Nights"—
"Ali Baba and the 40 thieves," "Abu Keer and Abu Seer," and
"Aladdin and the magic lamp."
ISBN-13: 978-0-8027-9639-4 • ISBN-10: 0-8027-9639-7
[1. Fairy tales. 2. Arabs—Folklore. 3. Folklore—Arab countries.]
1. Pohrt, Tom, ill. II. Arabian nights. English. Selections. 2007. III. Title.
PZ8.M6955Gen2007 398.2—dc22 2006027620

Visit Walker & Company's Web site at www.walkeryoungreaders.com

The illustrations for this book were created with pen and ink.

Book design by Amy Manzo Toth
Typeset by Westchester Book Composition
Printed in the U.S.A. by Quebecor World Farfield
2 4 6 8 10 9 7 5 3 1

All papers used by Walker & Company are natural, recyclable products
made from wood grown in well-managed forests. The manufacturing processes
conform to the environmental regulations of the country of origin.

To Race Andrade and to Travis Robinson —*S. M.*

For Isabel and Carmen —*T. P.*

Contents

Genies, Meanies, and Magic Rings

Ali Baba and the Forty Thieves

CHAPTER 1

A VERY LONG time ago, in a town in Persia, there lived two brothers whose names were Kassim and Ali Baba.

When their father died, he left them hardly any money. Kassim married a rich wife and became a famous merchant. But Ali Baba married a poor girl. He earned his living by cutting firewood

in the forest and selling it at the bazaar. Every morning he would lead his three donkeys to the forest, and every afternoon he would lead them back to town, piled high with wood. It was a modest living, but he and his wife were happy with very little.

One day, as Ali Baba was cutting wood at the edge of a thicket, with his donkeys grazing nearby, he heard the sound of galloping horses. A large cloud of dust was approaching fast. He hid his donkeys and climbed up a tree, just to be safe. From high up, he saw a troop of horsemen, armed with swords and spears, charging toward him. They looked ferocious, and he was ice-cold with fear. He counted. There were forty of them.

They galloped up to the tree Ali Baba was hiding in, jumped down from their horses, unfastened their saddlebags, heavy with

gold and silver, and carried them to a large rock at the bottom of the hill. It was obvious that they had just robbed a rich caravan.

After all the thieves had dropped off their saddlebags, a tall, muscular man who seemed to be their captain walked to the rock and shouted, "Open, Sesame!"

Immediately there was an empty space in the rock, as if a hidden door had swung open. Ali Baba watched in astonishment as the thieves entered and the rock closed behind them. In a few minutes they walked out, with empty saddlebags. Again the rock closed behind them. Then the forty thieves leaped up onto their horses and galloped off in a cloud of dust.

After a long while, when Ali Baba thought it was safe, he climbed down from the tree and walked over to the rock. He moved his hands over every inch of its surface. It was hard and jagged, like an ordinary rock, with no trace of a door. Then he stepped back and shouted, "Open, Sesame!" The rock opened. He walked in, and it closed behind him.

The cave wasn't dank and dismal, as he'd expected. It was actually quite well lit, from an opening in the top of the rock. As he looked around he could see a treasure so vast that it made him catch his breath. Gold and silver coins were heaped in huge piles, from floor to ceiling, and sacks bursting with precious stones, gold ingots in ten-foot-tall stacks, sculpted lamps and bowls made of solid gold, diamond necklaces, bracelets of emeralds and rubies, bales of the richest silks and brocades, and priceless carpets were piled high in every corner of the cave. Ali Baba stared and stared. A shiver of awe ran through his body.

As his astonishment gave way to thought, he realized that this cave must have been a thieves' storeroom for generation after generation. All the gold and jewels piled up around him must have been stolen or robbed, and many of the owners had probably been murdered in the process. Ali Baba felt afraid, but excited, too. *As long as I'm here*, he thought, *and God has led me to discover this place of crime, I might as well take some of the treasure home with me. It doesn't seem wrong. After all, there's no way to find out who are the rightful owners and give it back to them.*

So he took six large bags of gold coins, slung them over his shoulder one at a time, since each one was very heavy, and carried them out of the cave. He loaded them onto his donkeys and covered the bags with wood, so that no one would suspect what he was carrying. Then he waited in the forest until dusk.

When Ali Baba arrived home that night, he unloaded the donkeys, carried the six large bags of gold, one by one, into his house, and emptied the bags onto the floor. His wife stared, bewildered, at the immense pile of gold.

"Where did this come from?" was all she could say at first. Then she began to cry. "I would rather be poor," she sobbed, "than have you steal even a penny."

"Don't be upset," Ali Baba said. "I haven't done anything wrong. God guided my footsteps in the forest this morning, and that's how I discovered this treasure." Then he told her about his adventure.

When she heard his explanation, she breathed a long sigh of relief. "Thank God!" she said, and she began to cry again, her face bright with joy. After a while, she stopped crying and kneeled in front of the huge pile of gold coins that Ali Baba had poured out of the bags. She wanted to figure out how many coins there were.

"No, no, sweetheart, don't even try to count them," Ali Baba said. "It would take days. Let's just dig a large hole in the kitchen floor and bury them. If we leave them here, all the neighbors will be suspicious, and we're sure to get into trouble."

But his wife wanted to know exactly how rich they had become. "Maybe there are too many gold coins to count," she said. "But at least I can weigh them. I'm going to borrow a scale from your brother. And while you're digging the hole, I'll weigh the coins."

She walked over to Kassim's house and asked his wife to lend her a scale.

"Of course," said Kassim's wife. But she smelled a rat. After all, why would Ali Baba need a scale? He was so poor that he earned only a day's supply of wheat at a time. What kind of grain could he possibly have that needed to be weighed? So she rubbed a little fat onto the bottom of the wooden scale and hoped that some grain would stick to it.

Ali Baba's wife walked back home and weighed the gold. The pile was so large that this took her many hours. When she returned the scale to Kassim's wife the next day, she was exhausted, and she didn't notice that one small coin had stuck to the fat at the bottom.

"Aha!" said Kassim's wife as she spied the gold coin. "So *that's* what they've been weighing! They must have so much gold that they can't even count it!" She felt sick with envy.

She sent a slave to her husband's shop, with the message to come home right away. When Kassim came home, she screamed out the story. "I'll just shrivel up and die if they're

richer than we are. Find out how much gold they have and how they got it. There must be *something* we can do!"

Kassim, too, felt sick with envy. He hurried to Ali Baba's house and stormed in.

"So! You're as poor as a mouse, are you?" he said. "You liar! What about this, hmm?" And he took out the gold coin. "You're filthy rich! You have so much gold that you can't even count the coins! Now tell me how you got it, or I'll go straight to the police!"

Ali Baba told Kassim the whole story—how he had seen the thieves, entered the cave, and taken a tiny part of the treasure. "But please, *please*," he said at the end, "keep it a secret, or who knows what trouble we'll get into."

As he hurried home, Kassim felt as if his brain were on fire. *Why should my fool of a brother have all the luck?* he thought. *I'll go with* ten *donkeys and find the treasure and take it all for myself!*

His wife felt the same way. "That's the *least* we can do!" she said. "We deserve it more than anyone else. We'll be the richest people in town!"

CHAPTER 3

Early the next morning Kassim took his ten donkeys, each carrying two enormous boxes, and crept out of town. He hurried through the forest and soon came to the rock that Ali Baba had described. "Here it is!" he said to himself, as he rubbed his hands with glee. He could almost smell the gold. After tethering the donkeys to some nearby trees, he stood in front of the rock and shouted, "Open, Sesame!" and the rock opened wide, exactly as Ali Baba had told him it would. He walked in, and the rock closed behind him.

Inside the cave Kassim could hardly believe the size of the thieves' fabulous treasure. It was beyond his wildest dreams. He tried to guess how many trips it would take him, with his ten donkeys, to carry it all back home. But this turned out to be too much to figure out, so he gave up and went to work. He took twenty of the largest bags of jewels and dragged them to the entrance. Then he stood and shouted, "Open, Timothy!"

The rock didn't open.

Wait a minute, he said to himself. *Ali Baba told me to repeat the same password as when I was outside the cave. Why isn't the rock opening?* He scratched his head and thought for a moment. *Maybe I got the word a little wrong. It's the name of a plant. I know that. And it has three syllables. Okay. Now I remember*. And he shouted, "Open, Sassafras!"

The rock still didn't open.

He was getting scared now. He shouted, "Open, Tarragon!"

Still no movement.

He shouted, "Open, Tamarind!"

Nothing.

By now he realized, with horror, that he had completely forgotten the magic words. Desperately he shouted, "Open, Samasar! Open, Sarasit! Open, Tamasee! Open, Semasoo!"

As Kassim was shouting, the forty thieves galloped up to the cave.

They jumped down from their horses, and when they saw the ten donkeys, they drew their blades. Their captain pointed to the rock and said the magic words. The rock opened, and there was Kassim, trembling with terror.

The captain walked up to him and calmly lifted his razor-sharp sword, then brought it down through Kassim's skull and body as easily as a hot knife slices through a stick of butter. Then the thieves cut his body into four pieces and hung it up just inside the cave as a warning to other intruders.

CHAPTER 4

When evening came and Kassim still hadn't returned home, his wife began to worry. In a few hours she was frantic. She ran to Ali Baba's house and begged him to go look for his brother. Ali Baba took his three donkeys and left.

It was sunrise by the time he arrived at the cave. He said the magic words, the rock opened, and he walked in. As soon as he saw Kassim's body he knew what had happened. A wave of nausea and grief welled up inside him. But he had to act quickly. He put the pieces of the body into two empty bags and loaded these onto one donkey. Then he dragged out four more bags of gold, loaded them onto the other donkeys, and covered them with wood.

When he arrived home, he left the two donkeys with the gold at home and led the other one to his brother's house. He knocked at the door. It was opened by Marjanah, the brightest of his brother's slaves.

"I really need your help, Marjanah," he said. "Your master is dead; he was hacked apart by thieves. We've *got* to keep this a secret. We've got to bury him so that no one suspects what has happened."

Then he told the bad news to Kassim's wife. "It's a terrible tragedy, dear sister," he said. "But it is God's will. We will come live with you, if that makes it easier to bear. God has given us more wealth than we can possibly use; we'll be glad to share it all with you. But no one must discover our secret."

The next morning Marjanah went to the druggist's shop. "I need your strongest medicine," she said.

"Who's sick?" the druggist asked.

"My master," said Marjanah. "He woke up this morning paralyzed. He can't even talk. It's awful."

The druggist gave her an herb that was used only for the most serious illnesses.

In the afternoon Marjanah returned to the druggist's shop with tears in her eyes. "He's even worse," she said. "Isn't there anything stronger you can give him?"

The druggist thought for a moment. "Yes," he said. "But are you sure he's worse?"

"Oh, much worse," Marjanah said. "He's barely breathing. His skin is almost blue."

"That's not a good sign," the druggist said. "Here. Give him this. It's only for patients on the brink of death."

"Thank you," Marjanah said, sniffling. "But I'm afraid it's too late."

Word of Kassim's illness had spread from the druggist to all the neighbors. That evening no one was surprised to hear, coming from Kassim's house, the shrieks and sobs of Marjanah, Kassim's wife, and Ali Baba's wife.

The next morning Marjanah went to the shop of Mustafa, an old tailor in another part of town where nobody knew her.

"I have a job for you," she said. "It's for a very important person who wishes it to be done in secret. Bring your needles and thread along. I'm supposed to blindfold you and take you to his house."

"I'm sorry," Mustafa said. "This job sounds too fishy. I won't have anything to do with it."

"He is a *very* important person," Marjanah said, slipping a gold coin into the tailor's hand.

"Hmm," said Mustafa. "Perhaps it isn't all *that* fishy."

Marjanah gave him another gold coin.

"In fact, it doesn't seem fishy at all," Mustafa said. "I'll do it."

"Good," said Marjanah. "I assure you that you'll be well rewarded for your trouble."

After leading Mustafa through the streets to Ali Baba's house, she took off the blindfold and showed him the four pieces of Kassim's body. Then she gave him another gold coin and said, "Sew these together. If you finish in an hour, I'll give you more gold."

The old man worked quickly, and before long he had sewn the parts together so neatly that the stitches were practically invisible. Marjanah put the blindfold on him again, led him back to his shop, and swore him to secrecy.

Then she hurried home and made all the preparations for

Kassim's funeral. He was buried, and no one ever suspected what had really happened.

During the next few days Ali Baba and his wife moved to Kassim's house, taking their few possessions with them. At night Ali Baba moved the bags of gold and hid them in a corner of Kassim's cellar. Kassim's oldest son was put in charge of his father's shop.

CHAPTER 5

When the forty thieves returned to their cave, they were shocked to find that someone had taken Kassim's body. They also noticed that several bags of gold were missing.

"Men," said the captain, "this is serious. Not only does someone know the magic words, but he has had the nerve to steal our warning, right from under our noses. If things continue like this, we'll lose our whole treasure. This thief must be found and punished—quickly!"

He stood silent for a few moments. Suddenly he had an idea. "You!" he shouted to one of the thieves. "Go into town and spy for us. Ask around. The first thing we need to know is the name of that fellow we chopped up."

Before sunrise the next morning the spy walked into town. The first shop he saw happened to be Mustafa the tailor's.

"Good morning," he said cheerfully.

"Morning," Mustafa said.

"Looks like it'll be a fine day," he continued.

"Yes, it does," Mustafa said.

"You start work awfully early, don't you?" the spy said. "You must have wonderful eyesight to see so well before it's even light out."

"God be praised, I do," said Mustafa. "I can still thread a needle the first time I try. Why, just yesterday I sewed together a mutilated corpse in a dark cellar. I didn't even have a candle." Then, remembering his vow of secrecy, he said, "Oops!"

"What's wrong?" the spy said.

"I wasn't supposed to say that," Mustafa said. "I was sworn to secrecy."

"But you haven't really told me a thing," the spy said. "Anyway, I'm very impressed. And to show that you can trust me, here's a gold coin for you. By the way, whose body was it?"

"I have no idea," Mustafa said, pocketing the gold coin. "I was blindfolded and led to a house by a girl. Then, after I sewed up the corpse, she blindfolded me again and brought me back."

"I am quite curious about this house," said the spy, slipping another gold coin into the tailor's hand. "I'd very much appreciate it if you could take me there. Why don't we do this: I'll blindfold you, and you can lead me along the route you took yesterday. There's more gold waiting for you if you succeed."

Blindfolded, Mustafa held on to the spy's sleeve and groped his way to Ali Baba's house.

"Here it is," he said. "This is the place."

The spy removed the blindfold, gave him another gold coin, and sent him on his way.

Then he took a piece of chalk out of his pocket and scrawled a large X on Ali Baba's door. *All right, smart aleck*, he thought. *Now you're done for*. And he returned to the forest as quickly as he could and told his captain the news.

"Good work!" the captain said. "Tomorrow we'll go into town and kill everyone in the house."

CHAPTER 6

That afternoon, when Marjanah went out to do the day's shopping, she noticed the chalk X on the door. *This is strange,* she thought. *Why would someone put a mark on our door? It can't be for any honest reason, or they would have told us about it. Something suspicious is going on here, and I'd better do something about it.*

So she got a piece of chalk and drew a large X on every door in the neighborhood.

The next morning, with their spy in the lead, the thieves arrived at Ali Baba's street. But every door on the street had a large X chalked on it.

"What is the meaning of this?" whispered the captain, furious.

"I can't understand it, sir," whispered the spy. "I know I marked just one of the doors."

"You incompetent fool!" whispered the captain. "Take him back, men, and smash his skull. There isn't a brain inside it, anyway."

The next day the captain himself rode into town, straight to the tailor, who led him to Ali Baba's house. He stood in front of it for a long time, until he knew every grain in its wood and every scratch on its doorknob. Then he returned to the forest.

He called the thieves together (there were thirty-eight of them now, plus the captain). "All right, men," he said, "I know which house the intruder lives in. And tomorrow's the day of our sweet revenge. I have a plan. Each one of you bring me a large urn, big enough for a man to fit into. Plus one extra. I'll explain the rest to you later."

The thieves rode off to the bazaar and returned with thirty-nine urns. The captain, who had put on robes of the finest silk to disguise himself as a rich merchant, ordered them to fill one of these with oil. "The rest of the urns will be empty," he said, "and you will be inside them. I will get the intruder to invite us into his house. Sometime after dinner, I will find an excuse to go out into the courtyard. I will knock once on each of the urns. That will be the signal for you to come out. We'll storm the

house and slit the throats of everyone in it. But until you hear the signal, stay put inside the urns."

Then he gave each of his men a knife, had each one tie an empty urn onto his horse, and climb into the urn. He covered each urn with a thin cloth, so that the men would be hidden, yet able to breathe. Finally he led the horses into town.

When he came to Ali Baba's house, the captain found him sitting on the front step, enjoying the mild evening air.

"Good evening, sir," said the captain, bowing.

"Good evening," Ali Baba said.

"I am a stranger here," the captain continued, smiling. "I came to sell my oil at the bazaar, but I arrived too late and don't

have anywhere to spend the night. Would you be kind enough to let me and my horses rest in the courtyard of your house? I would be most grateful to you."

"Of course," said Ali Baba. "Hospitality to strangers is a sacred duty. You are welcome here, sir."

Ali Baba took the captain's arm and led him into the house. "Marjanah!" he called. "Come here. We have a stranger who will be staying with us tonight. Tell the others to unload those big urns of oil and feed the horses. And make a special dinner for our honored visitor and see that the guest room is prepared with everything he might need."

As Marjanah was in the kitchen cooking dinner, her lamp suddenly ran out of oil.

This is ridiculous, she thought. *Here we are, with no oil in the house, while just outside are dozens of huge urns filled with oil. Our guest certainly won't mind if I borrow a little from him until tomorrow morning.*

Holding the lamp, she walked out into the courtyard, to the place where the thirty-nine urns had been put. She knocked on one of the urns to see how full it was. A voice whispered, "Is it time?"

In a flash Marjanah understood exactly what was happening and whispered, "Not yet!" She knocked on each urn, and each urn whispered, "Is it time?" And to each question she whispered, "Not yet!"

Her heart was racing. She knew that Ali Baba and his whole family were in great danger, and if she didn't do something quickly, they would all be dead. But what could she do? If even

one of these villains was allowed to live, they might come back and kill someone. Ah, the oil! Boiling oil would be one way to kill them. The last urn was filled with oil, so she took several bucketfuls from it and went back to the kitchen. Then she poured the oil into a large cauldron and put it on the fire. When the oil was boiling hot, she went out to the courtyard and poured it into the urns, one by one. The thieves were scalded to death.

After dinner the captain walked out into the courtyard and knocked on one of the urns. Not a sound came from it.

He knocked on a second urn. Still no sound.

These filthy dogs! he thought. *They've fallen asleep on me!* But when he touched the urns they were hot, and he smelled the odor of burnt flesh.

Someone has killed them, he said to himself. *He must be lying in wait for me, too. I'd better get out of here!* So he jumped over the courtyard wall and ran back to the forest.

Marjanah took Ali Baba out to the courtyard and had him look into the urns. Each one contained a body. Ali Baba almost threw up. But he was happy to know that the thieves were dead, and very grateful to Marjanah for her courage and quick wit.

"Dear, dear Marjanah," he said, with tears in his eyes. "This is the second time in two days that you have saved our lives. From now on, you will no longer be our slave, but our own beloved daughter."

They buried the thirty-eight bodies in a large hole in the yard. And for the next five years, Ali Baba and his family lived in happiness and peace.

By now Ali Baba's oldest nephew had made a great success with Kassim's shop and had become a rich merchant. One day he said to his uncle, "You have never met my dear friend Hassan. It's been six months since he opened the shop next to mine, and he's been so kind and generous to me that I'd love to do something nice for him. May I invite him over for a feast in his honor?"

"Of course!" said Ali Baba. "Any friend of yours is a friend of mine. We'll prepare a splendid feast."

The feast was spread on the table. All the guests were seated and talking cheerfully when Marjanah came in from the kitchen with a golden platter of delicacies. When she looked at Hassan, she shuddered. *I've seen that man before,* she thought. *Who can he be? He looks awfully familiar*. And suddenly, to her horror, she realized that Hassan was none other than the thieves' captain, whom they hadn't seen for years and had almost forgotten. He had a knife tucked into his belt; even though it was well hidden, she could see the glint of the steel.

When the feast was over, Marjanah again entered the room, this time dressed as a dancer. Ali Baba was a little surprised; they hadn't planned any entertainment. But everyone enjoyed Marjanah's dance. It was a traditional dance about a warrior woman. Around and around she twirled, with the ceremonial dagger in her left hand. Hassan, who liked anything that had to do with war and warriors, was especially delighted, and he took out his purse to get a gold coin for her. As he bent forward she rushed up to him and stabbed him in the heart.

"What have you done?!" Ali Baba screamed.

"You must be crazy!" shrieked the nephew. "You've murdered my best friend!"

"Look!" Marjanah said. And she tore off the merchant's belt. The knife fell to the floor.

"Don't you remember?" she said, pointing at his face. "It's the captain of the thieves! He came here to kill you!"

"Dear Marjanah," Ali Baba said, taking her into his arms. "Once again you have saved us. How can I reward you? Ask for anything you want."

Marjanah blushed. "I already have everything I want. I have a wonderful home here, and I really do feel like your daughter." Then she looked down at the ground.

"Nephew," Ali Baba said to Kassim's oldest son, "can *you* think of anything our dear Marjanah might want?"

"Well, Uncle," he said, "if she loves me as much as I love her, perhaps she might want to marry me."

"That's an excellent idea," Ali Baba said. "Is this what you want, Marjanah?"

Marjanah blushed again and whispered, "Yes."

"Wonderful!" Ali Baba said. "There's nothing that would make me happier."

And so Marjanah married Ali Baba's nephew, and they were very happy with each other.

A year after the wedding, when Ali Baba felt that it was safe to return, he went back to the cave in the forest. The path was covered with long grass and was almost invisible. Obviously no one had been here for a long time. Ali Baba stood in front of the rock and shouted, "Open, Sesame!" And once again the rock opened.

After this, he made many trips to the cave, and he taught the secret to his children and his grandchildren.

So Ali Baba became the richest man of his time, and he used his wealth with great wisdom. Everyone blessed him and said, "He is fair to the rich and compassionate to the poor." And he and his family lived happily until the end of their days.

Abu Keer and Abu Seer

CHAPTER 1

A VERY LONG time ago, in the city of Alexandria in Egypt, there were two neighbors. One was a dyer named Abu Keer, the other a barber named Abu Seer. Their shops were right next to each other at the bazaar.

Now Abu Seer was a kind, honest man. But Abu Keer was a liar and a cheat. Whenever a customer brought him a piece of cloth to be dyed, he would insist on being paid in advance, and he would go out and spend the money on expensive food and wine and tobacco. Then he would sell the cloth and spend *that* money. And when the customer returned, he would say, "Come back tomorrow."

The next day he would say, "I'm terribly sorry, your cloth is still not ready. I had guests all day yesterday, and of course I had to entertain them. But it will be ready tomorrow, I promise."

The customer would return on the third day. Abu Keer would say, "Would you believe it?! My wife had a baby last

night, and I had to take care of her all day. But tomorrow your cloth will definitely be ready."

Things would go on like this until the customer ran out of patience and asked for his cloth back.

"Ah, if only I *could* return it to you," Abu Keer would say, looking down with tears in his eyes. Then he would pause and pretend to choke down a sob. "But God is just and will punish the wicked."

"What happened?" the customer would ask.

"Sir, I dyed your cloth yesterday. A beautiful job, if I may say so myself. You've never seen such an artistic dye job! Then I hung it out to dry. And—would you believe it?!—when I came back, the cloth wasn't there! Some filthy thief must have taken it!"

"Ah, well," the customer would sigh, if he was a kind man. "God is just and will make all things right." If he was a bad-tempered man, he would rage and curse and call Abu Keer every foul name under the sun. But the curses would bounce off Abu Keer like water off a raincoat.

In time, though, word got around, and people began to warn one another about Abu Keer's tricks. So his customers grew fewer and fewer, until there were no customers at all.

With nothing to do, Abu Keer began to hang around Abu Seer's shop, and the two became friends. Abu Seer hadn't heard any of the gossip. He considered Abu Keer to be a very clever man and enjoyed his conversation. Abu Seer was a loyal friend, and being an innocent, trustworthy person, he thought that his friends were as trustworthy as he was.

One day Abu Seer said to Abu Keer, "What terrible luck you have! Every time someone brings you a piece of cloth, it gets stolen. There must be more thieves in this town than ants at a picnic."

Abu Keer said, "I'll let you in on a secret, neighbor. Nobody has ever stolen a thing from me."

"Really? Then what happened to all that merchandise?"

"I sold it. You have no idea how delicious rich people's food can be! Stuffed nightingale tongues, mocha date-nut tarts . . . And the wines! They are like beautiful music playing on your tongue."

"But, neighbor!" Abu Seer interrupted. "Stealing is a crime! You can't pull the wool over *God's* eyes, you know."

"Ah," sighed Abu Keer. "I only steal because I'm so poor and business is so bad. I'm the best dyer in Alexandria. By all rights I should be rich. When you're rich, it's easy to be honest."

Abu Seer said, "I disagree with you, neighbor. I don't think it's ever right to steal. But business is terrible for me, too. I wish we could do something to improve it."

"Maybe we can," said Abu Keer. "Why don't we just leave this miserable city and see if we can find a better one? Maybe somewhere else they'll appreciate having a master dyer and a good barber."

So they agreed to travel and find a better home. They also agreed that whenever one of them had work and the other didn't, the one who was working would support the one who wasn't. And all the money left over as profit would be divided equally between them.

The very next morning they set sail.

Abu Keer immediately curled up in the cabin and went to sleep. Abu Seer, taking his equipment—scissors, razor, a basin of water, soap, and a towel—went out for a walk on the deck.

"Hey, barber! Over here!" one of the passengers shouted. Abu Seer cut his hair and shaved him. "How much will that be?" the passenger said.

"Well, my friend and I are hungry. If you can spare a loaf of bread . . ."

"Certainly," said the passenger. "It was such a good haircut that I'll even throw in a piece of cheese."

Pretty soon there was a line of people waiting for Abu Seer. By the end of the first day, he had earned thirty silver coins, thirty loaves of bread, and a pile of cheese, olives, and fruit.

When he brought his earnings back to the cabin, he found Abu Keer still asleep.

"Wake up, partner," he said. "Look what I have!"

Abu Keer got up and began to stuff the food into his mouth, as if he had been starving for a week. He ate seven loaves of bread, four large hunks of cheese, a hundred and forty-two olives, nine apples, three pears, three peaches, and a medium-sized bunch of grapes. Then he let out a loud belch and went back to sleep.

The next day there was another long line of customers for Abu Seer. Everyone on board, it seemed, wanted a haircut. In the afternoon, the ship's captain came. He was so pleased with his haircut and shave that he invited Abu Seer and his friend to join him for dinner every night for the rest of the voyage.

"Wake up, partner," Abu Seer said when he returned to the cabin with another load of food at the end of the day.

Abu Keer got up again and began to stuff the food into his mouth.

"No, wait," said Abu Seer. "The captain has invited us to dinner. Don't waste your appetite on this."

"You go by yourself," Abu Keer mumbled, his mouth full of bread and cheese. "I'm feeling seasick. Just remember to bring me some leftovers."

The captain's dinner was magnificent. There were twelve kinds of meat, including shish kebab and roast chicken, ten different vegetables, and two dozen desserts, including baklava and sherbet. Abu Seer had never eaten such delicious food. There were tears of gratitude in his eyes as he thanked the captain.

"By the way, sir," he continued, "I wonder if I may take back some leftovers for my friend."

"Of course," said the captain. "But didn't you say that he was feeling seasick?"

"Well," said Abu Seer, "maybe he's better by now. I would love it if he could taste this amazing food."

Back in the cabin Abu Keer was still eating the bread and cheese Abu Seer had brought him.

"I *told* you to save your appetite," Abu Seer said. "Look what I have for you."

Abu Keer said, "Hand it over!" and wolfed down the roast chicken and the lamb and the fish and the beef, the beans and the peas and the rice, the date cake and the almond cake. Not a single crumb was left. "Is this *all* you brought?" he snarled.

"I thought it would be enough," Abu Seer said. "It was a huge plateful, and you had just eaten."

"A fine friend *you* are!" Abu Keer said, snarling. Then he got into bed, rolled over, and went to sleep.

CHAPTER 3

Things continued like this for the next twenty days of the voyage. Every morning Abu Seer went off to work; every evening he brought back the day's profits. Abu Keer never woke up except to eat, and never left his bed except to go to the toilet.

On the twenty-first day, the ship docked in the harbor of a large city. Before Abu Seer left the ship, the captain took him aside and said, "Let me give you a piece of advice. Don't go to the king of this city unless you have something valuable to offer him. He is known for his short temper, and everyone is very careful around him because he wears a magic ring. Whenever he wants to kill anyone, all he has to do is point with his right hand, and immediately that person's head falls off, like a ripe melon falling off a vine."

"My goodness," Abu Seer said. "I'll certainly remember your advice. Thanks."

Once they had disembarked, Abu Keer and Abu Seer found

a cheap hotel and rented a room with a bed in it and a small cot. "I'll take the bed," Abu Keer said, and immediately went to sleep.

Every morning, for the next forty days, Abu Seer would go out, find a few customers, and return with food for dinner. He would cook it and serve it and clean up afterward. Abu Keer would wake up only long enough to gobble down a large meal. Whenever Abu Seer suggested that he look for work, Abu Keer would grumble, "Don't bother me," and he would go back to sleep.

Forty days went by like this. Then Abu Seer got sick and couldn't go out to work. He lay on his cot all day long, with a fever so high that he lost consciousness.

Abu Keer woke up that afternoon with pangs in his belly. "Where's my dinner?!" he roared. But Abu Seer was stretched out on his cot, unconscious, pale as a sheet.

Abu Keer got up and ate all the food he could find in the room, but he was still hungry. So he got dressed, searched through his friend's clothes, and found a dozen silver coins in one of his pockets. He took these and left.

First he went to a restaurant and had a thirteen-course meal that lasted for three hours. Then he walked to the bazaar and spent all the rest of the money on an expensive silk robe. As he walked through the streets he noticed that all the people were dressed in either white clothes or blue clothes, or else a mixture of white and blue. "Hmm," said Abu Keer to himself. "This is awfully peculiar."

Soon he came to a dyer's shop. All the material inside it was dyed blue.

Taking out a handkerchief, he said to the dyer, "I'd like this dyed."

"Yes, sir," the dyer said. "It will be ready tomorrow."

"Is that all?" said Abu Keer. "Don't you need to know what *color* I want it dyed?"

"Oh no, sir," the dyer said. "The only color I know how to dye is blue."

"Is that so?" Abu Keer said. "What about the other dyers in town?"

"It's the same with them, sir. There are forty-nine master dyers here, and we all use only blue dye. Besides, we know from experience that it's impossible to dye cloth any other color than blue."

"Is that so?" said Abu Keer, and he walked away with a smile on his face.

The very same day he went to see the king. "Your Majesty," he said, "I have just arrived here. I had heard of your magnificent city in Alexandria, where I was a master dyer. And indeed, your city is a most splendid capital, filled with more marvelous things than I could have imagined, a testimony to Your Majesty's wisdom and goodness. However, there is room for one tiny improvement."

"And what might that be?" the king said.

"Well, Your Most Gracious Majesty, I couldn't help noticing that your dyers work only in blue. Now wouldn't it be a wonderful benefit to you and your citizens if there were a dyer who could work in other colors?"

"Assuredly," the king said. "But where is such a genius to be found?"

"Your Majesty," said Abu Keer, "this is your lucky day. That genius is standing right before you! I can dye cloth red, green, blue, yellow, orange, purple, and brown. Do you want something dyed red? I can dye it the color of a rose or a cherry, a ruby or a sunset or a hummingbird's throat. Do you want something dyed green? I can dye it the green of a blade of grass or a pistachio nut or a cypress needle or an olive. Purple? I can dye it plum or violet or amethyst or lavender or heliotrope or lilac or magenta or mulberry. And even with blue—you have no idea how many beautiful shades of blue there are. Azure and aquamarine, cobalt and cerulean, indigo, hyacinth, periwinkle, peacock and turquoise and ultramarine. I am a modest man, Your Majesty, but if you will permit me to toot my own horn for a moment: in Alexandria even the other dyers call me the greatest dyer of our age."

"My goodness," said the king.

He was so impressed with Abu Keer that he gave him five

thousand gold coins, a diamond ring, a wardrobe of embroidered silk clothing (all of it white or blue), a large house with a rose garden, ten slaves, and a white horse. And he ordered his architects and carpenters to build him a luxurious shop in the best location in town. Within a few weeks, Abu Keer was in business.

The king sent him five hundred lengths of cloth, and Abu Keer dyed them every color of the rainbow. The king was astonished. When the cloths were displayed outside the shop, the people ooh'd and ahh'd. They had never seen anything so beautiful. Soon everyone in the country was bringing material to Abu Keer. The ministers of state brought their robes. The army officers brought their uniforms. Even poor shopkeepers brought their ragged business suits. And with the gold they paid, and the presents that the king kept showering upon him, Abu Keer quickly became a very wealthy man.

CHAPTER 5

Abu Seer remained unconscious on his cot in the hotel room for three days. Finally the hotel porter got worried, knocked on the door, and opened it. There lay Abu Seer, moaning.

"For the love of God, friend," he said, "get me something to eat. I'm so famished I could cry."

The porter rushed out and returned with a bowl of beef soup. He propped Abu Seer up and spoon-fed him until he had eaten all the soup.

"Thank you so much," said Abu Seer. "I feel better now."

"Where's your friend?" the porter asked.

"I don't know. He must have gone out to get me some medicine."

"But I haven't seen him for three days," the porter said.

"I don't understand," said Abu Seer. "I'm sure he wouldn't just leave me here sick as a dog. Anyway, please look in my pockets and take out a few coins for the soup. And if you could buy me some more food, I'd be very grateful."

The porter looked and said, “These pockets are empty. Your friend must have robbed you and left. Some friend!”

“Oh, he would never do that!” Abu Seer said. “He probably just took the money to buy some expensive medicine for me. I bet he’ll be back any minute.”

“Don’t hold your breath,” said the porter.

CHAPTER 6

For the next two months the porter took care of Abu Seer, paying for his food and medicine, and nursing him back to health.

Finally Abu Seer was well again.

"I'll never forget what you've done for me," he said to the porter. "If God ever gives me the means, I'll repay you a thousand times over for your kindness."

"Thank you," said the porter. "But that's not necessary. Seeing you healthy again is reward enough."

Abu Seer walked out of the hotel and into the delicious summer air. It felt wonderful to be outdoors again.

Soon he came to the bazaar and noticed a shop with a display of beautifully dyed cloths and a large crowd in front. He asked one of the men in the crowd what was going on, and the man told him about Abu Keer's fabulous success.

"Praise be to God," Abu Seer said to himself, "for allowing

my friend to prosper so greatly. He has been busy with all these customers, and the king, too. No wonder he forgot about me. But everything will be all right now. When he wasn't feeling well, I took care of him, and now he'll do the same for me."

Abu Seer threaded his way through the crowd and slipped in at the front door. He could hardly believe his eyes. There, on a pile of velvet cushions in the middle of the shop, sat Abu Keer in his embroidered silk robes, looking as mighty as a king and as comfortable as a cat. Four black slaves, four white slaves, and four Asian slaves, all dressed in gorgeous uniforms of silk and satin, were continually moving toward and away from him, sometimes kneeling to fan him or polish his nails or play his favorite music or feed him candied oranges or chocolate-dipped

strawberries. Twenty-five more slaves were scurrying around, trying to keep up with his orders.

Abu Seer walked up to him and bowed. "It's been a long time, partner," he said.

"How *dare* you!" Abu Keer screamed. "How dare you, you insolent thief! Slaves, seize him!"

Six slaves pinned Abu Seer to the ground. Then Abu Keer took a whip and lashed him a dozen times on his back, then another dozen times on his stomach. When he had finished, Abu Seer was a mass of bleeding welts.

"That ought to teach you a lesson," shouted Abu Keer. "If you ever set foot here again, I'll have you arrested!"

"What did he do?" a customer asked.

"He's a filthy thief," Abu Keer said. "I don't know how many times he's stolen merchandise from me. 'God forgive him,' I say to myself, because he's a poor man. I keep warning him. But once a thief, always a thief. If he comes back, I'm going to hand him over to the police."

Bewildered, humiliated, and aching all over, Abu Seer stumbled back to the hotel. It took a week for him to recover.

CHAPTER 7

When the welts had stopped hurting, Abu Seer went out again. He wanted to treat himself to a long, relaxing soak in a hot bath, so he asked the first person he met to direct him to the public baths.

"The public paths?" said the man. "You mean for taking a walk?"

"No, not paths. *Baths!*"

"Baths? What are they?"

"*You* know," Abu Seer said. "Baths. Where people go to wash themselves."

"Oh," said the man. "You must be a stranger here. We call it the sea."

"You mean you have no hot baths here?"

"Never heard of such a thing," the man said.

Hmm, thought Abu Seer.

That very same day he went to the king. He was very

confident. Magic ring or no magic ring, he knew that he had a valuable idea to offer.

"Your Majesty," he said, "I have come here from far away, and I have been wondering why you don't have any public baths in this beautiful city."

"What are baths?" asked the king.

"Well," Abu Seer said, "they're hot and wonderful, and people go there to wash themselves clean, or for a massage, or just to sit and soak in a tub of hot water. It's one of the greatest pleasures in the world."

"My goodness," said the king.

He was so impressed with Abu Seer's idea that he gave him ten thousand gold coins and the use of the royal architects, carpenters, and stonemasons to build a bathhouse suitable for a great kingdom.

Soon Abu Seer had built a magnificent bathhouse. It was two stories high, patterned with green, blue, and white stones, and had marble columns all around it. Precious carpets covered the floors, there were three large marble fountains, dozens of potted orange and lemon trees perfumed the air, and the walls were bright with mosaics depicting flowers, birds, and animals of every variety.

After being greeted by Abu Seer in the reception hall, a customer entered the shower room, where attendants would soap and scrub and shampoo him, rinse him off, and lead him to the main hall. Here there was a choice of five large red-marble pools, each one filled with water of a different temperature, from lukewarm to very hot. Once he had soaked to his heart's delight, he could shower and leave, or go to the massage room, where one of a staff of six male and female slaves, carefully trained by Abu Seer, would knead away all his aches and pains

and soothe him with sweet-smelling oils. In the center of the main hall, mineral water bubbled from the mouths of marble lions. Nearby, a quartet of musicians played beautiful, soothing music. Waiters walked back and forth, carrying silver trays of sherbets and cookies.

Abu Seer sent out criers to announce the grand opening of the bathhouse and invite everyone to come, free of charge, for three days.

No one had ever seen anything like it. Rich and poor alike were astonished at the magnificence of the bathhouse and overwhelmed with the pleasure of the baths. When they left, they were all glowing like fireflies.

On the fourth day, the king paid a visit, escorted by four hundred of his ministers, diplomats, generals, and noblemen—all the important members of his court. He soaked for an hour in the pool of lukewarm water, then for another hour in the next pool, an hour in the next, then the next, and finally for an hour in the hottest pool. Then he had a long massage. He came out scented with essence of white roses.

Abu Seer was waiting for him in the reception hall. Two white slave girls and two black slave girls, each one as beautiful as the full moon, brought in sherbets and cookies.

"Well, Your Majesty," Abu Seer said, "how do you like the baths?"

"Mmmmm," said the king. "I thought I was in heaven." He smiled and heaved a sigh of pleasure. Then he said, "You shall be well rewarded for this. How much, by the way, are you going to charge?"

"Whatever you think is fair, Your Majesty," said Abu Seer.

"A thousand gold coins. That is the very least you should charge for such a magnificent experience."

"You are very kind, Your Majesty," Abu Seer said, "but if you'll forgive me, I think that price is a bit steep. After all, some of your subjects are rich and some of them are poor. And if I charge a thousand gold coins for a bath, only the very rich will be able to afford it."

"Ah," said the king. "You are right. I didn't think of that. What shall we do, then?"

"Why don't we have a sliding scale?" Abu Seer said. "Everybody will pay what he can afford. You, Your Majesty, are a king, for example, so you can easily pay a thousand gold coins, as you suggested. Your courtiers and noblemen are rich, so they will pay a hundred gold coins. A poor fisherman or shoemaker, on the other hand, will pay just one copper penny. And a beggar won't have to pay a thing."

"Splendid!" said the king. "Now everybody will be able to afford these wonderful baths."

"I think that's the fairest way," Abu Seer said.

"And to express my gratitude," the king said, "I will give you an additional hundred thousand gold coins."

"Your Majesty's generosity is overwhelming," Abu Seer said. "A hundred thousand thanks."

The first thing Abu Seer did was to send for the hotel porter. He gave him fifty thousand gold coins. "Whenever you need anything," he said, "just come and ask me."

So Abu Seer became a very wealthy man, and a respected and well-liked citizen. Everyone in the city, from the king down to the poorest beggar, went for a bath once a week, and everyone walked out of the bathhouse beaming with pleasure. Abu Seer came to know all the king's advisers and all the members of his bodyguard. He was especially friendly with the king's admiral, and he wouldn't allow him to pay even a penny for his visits. "You're a good fellow," Abu Seer would say. "It's on the house."

CHAPTER 9

One day Abu Keer decided to go to the baths. As he walked into the reception hall he immediately recognized Abu Seer. *Ah*, he thought, *the bathhouse owner everyone is talking about is that wretched barber I used to know. I'd better do some fast talking.*

When Abu Seer saw him, he embraced him with joy.

"Shame on you!" Abu Keer said. "It's months since we arrived in this city, and I've become a rich man and a friend of the king. Yet you never visit me, you never even come by to say hello. Is that any way to treat an old friend?"

Abu Seer's mouth dropped in amazement.

"And I've worn myself out searching for you," Abu Keer continued. "I've sent my slaves all over the city, to every rooming house and hotel. But there wasn't even a shred of news about you. You had disappeared into thin air."

"But don't you remember?" said Abu Seer. "I *came* to your shop. And you called me a thief and whipped me!" He had tears in his eyes.

"Oh my God!" Abu Keer said, pretending to be shocked. "Was that *you*?"

Abu Seer nodded.

"I had no idea," Abu Keer said. "Believe me, dear friend, I had absolutely no idea it was you. I swear to God, I swear by the beard of the prophet Mohammed, I swear by my father's prayer rug, I swear by my mother's apron strings, that I didn't recognize you. There was a dirty little thief who used to come every day and steal merchandise from my shop. He looked exactly like you. What a horrible mistake!"

"Really?" said Abu Seer.

"May God strike me dead if it isn't true," Abu Keer said. "I'm so sorry I didn't recognize you. My dear old friend! My dear, dear friend! Oh, how could I have been so blind?" By now Abu Keer was sobbing and beating his breast.

"There, there," said Abu Seer, patting him on the back. "It's all right. I forgive you."

They spent the next few hours soaking together in the hot pool and catching up on each other's news.

Finally Abu Keer offered one copper coin in payment.

"No, no," said Abu Seer. "You're my friend. It's on the house."

"Good," Abu Keer said. "You know, this is a fine place you have here. There's only one thing missing."

"What's that?" said Abu Seer.

"The massage oil we used to have in Alexandria, in our neighborhood baths."

"You mean that smelly stuff?"

"It may be smelly," said Abu Keer, "but it's wonderful massage oil. It makes you tingle all over. Why don't you get some of it and rub it on the king the next time he comes? I'm sure he'll appreciate it, and you'll rise even higher in his esteem."

"That sounds like a good idea," said Abu Seer. "A thousand thanks, old friend."

CHAPTER 10

Upon leaving the bathhouse, Abu Keer went straight to the king.

"How are you, Your Majesty?" he said.

"Wonderful, just wonderful!" said the king, smiling.

"Oh?"

"Yes, ever since that genius Abu Seer opened his bathhouse, I've been feeling on top of the world. I have never felt happier in my whole life."

"You mean, you've actually *gone* to the bathhouse?" said Abu Keer, with a look of deep concern.

"Of course I have," said the king. "Why are you looking at me that way?"

"God be praised that Your Majesty escaped!" Abu Keer said.

"What are you talking about?" the king said.

"Don't you know?" said Abu Keer. "That bath manager, Abu What's-his-name, is a crook!"

"No!" said the king.

"Not only is he a crook," Abu Keer said, "but he's an enemy of our holy religion. If you go to the baths after today, you're a dead man."

"Why?"

"It gives me great pain to say this," said Abu Keer, "because I used to know the man, but it's all a plot against Your Majesty's life. He wormed his way into your favor, built the bathhouse, and got you to enjoy the baths—all so that you'd trust him. It's a setup. The next time you go there, he's going to have an evil potion ready for you. He'll call it massage oil. But it's really poison. It will make you scream with agony, and within the hour you'll be dead."

"But why would he want to kill me?" asked the king.

"Well," Abu Keer said, "it's like this. Four years ago this villain and I went on a business trip to Spain, with his whole family. While we were traveling north, we were captured by the king of the Christians. But because the king saw that I have a very honest face, he let me open a dye shop. And, of course, he was so amazed at the quality of my work that he gave me my freedom.

"So I returned to Alexandria and then came here to your illustrious city. To my surprise, whom did I run into yesterday but this villain, Abu What's-his-name! He told me that shortly after I left, the king of the Christians had a big meeting and let all the prisoners attend. The meeting was about you, Your Majesty. The king said that you were his enemy, and that you were a dangerous man and an infidel, and that if anyone succeeded in killing you, he would be given whatever his heart desired. This Abu What's-his-name stepped forward and volunteered. The deal is this: If he kills you, the king of the Christians will set free his wife and children. And tomorrow is the big day," he said. "If it weren't for me, Your Majesty, and if it weren't for the great love I bear you, I'm afraid your goose would be cooked."

"I don't believe it," said the king. "He seems like such a kind man."

"He's cunning. *Very* cunning, Your Majesty," Abu Keer said.

"I still can't believe it," said the king, shaking his head.

"If I'm lying, Your Majesty," said Abu Keer, "may God strike me dead on the spot. Just go to the baths and *see* if he doesn't try to rub you with that evil-smelling poison! That will be the proof."

CHAPTER 11

The next morning the king went to the bathhouse.

"Good morning, Your Majesty," Abu Seer said.

"Good morning," said the king.

"This morning I have a special treat for you, Your Majesty."

"Oh?" said the king.

"Yes, it's a wonderful massage oil we used to have in Alexandria. It will make you tingle all over."

The king took one whiff of the oil and shouted, "Guards! Seize him!"

They grabbed Abu Seer and tied him up. Then the king called for his admiral.

"Take this villain," said the king. "Stuff him in a bag, fill it with rocks, and throw it into the sea! The sooner the better!"

"Aye-aye, Your Majesty!" said the admiral. "And where in the sea would you like him thrown, Your Majesty?"

"Right outside my palace," the king said. "I will be sitting in the window, waiting for you to row by. Just shout up to me, 'Now?' And I will shout, 'Now!' Then you can heave him in. And I hope that he drowns slowly and painfully."

The admiral took Abu Seer to a small island facing the king's palace, untied him, took the gag from his mouth, and said, "Tell me, old friend, what in the world did you do to deserve this punishment?"

"As God is my witness, I don't have the faintest idea," said Abu Seer.

"Hmm," said the admiral. "Either you're lying, or the king has gone crazy, or someone is plotting against you."

"I can't understand it," said Abu Seer, with tears in his eyes.

"Well," the admiral said, "I have seen court politics, and it looks as if there's foul play going on here. Someone's trying to ruin you—probably someone who envies your success. I believe you, so I'm going to let you go, even if I am risking my life by doing it. You just lie low on this island. Don't let anyone see you. We'll stop the first ship that docks here and send you off on it. No one will ever know."

"Thank you, dear friend," said Abu Seer, kissing the admiral's hand. "But what will you tell the king?"

"Oh, I've got that figured out," the admiral said. "I'll just put a large rock inside the bag, a rock as big as a man, and throw *that* overboard."

"Ah," said Abu Seer.

"One more thing," said the admiral. "One of my jobs is to provide fish for the royal kitchen. But with this errand, I'm not going to have time for fishing today. Would you do me a favor and go out with this fishing net? You've been lucky once today; maybe you'll be lucky again."

"I'd be glad to," Abu Seer said, taking the net. "And I'll remember not to let anyone see me."

The admiral found a huge rock, put it in the bag, and sailed in front of the window where the king sat.

"Now?" he shouted.

"Now!" shouted the king, with a flick of his hand. The movement was so abrupt that it shook loose the magic ring on his middle finger, and off it flew, down into the sea.

The king knew he was in trouble now. If his enemies found out that he had lost his magic ring, they would realize that he had lost his power, and they would arrest him and put him to death.

Meanwhile, Abu Seer was having wonderful luck. Every time he pulled in his net, it was full. By now he had a large heap of wriggling fish in front of him.

"I might as well have one for lunch," he said to himself, and he chose a nice fat fish. He cut off its head, but when he slit its belly, his knife hit against something hard.

That's strange, he thought, and opened up the fish. There was a ring inside its belly.

Beautiful! thought Abu Seer, and he put it on, without knowing that it was the magic ring.

Just then, two cooks from the royal kitchen arrived.

"Hey, you!" they shouted. "Where's the admiral?"

"He's not here," Abu Seer said.

"We know *that*, you moron. Where has he gone? He's supposed to give us some fish."

"Oh, he went that way," said Abu Seer, pointing toward

them. Immediately both their heads fell off. They hit the ground with a thud, rolled a little, and stopped.

Dear God! Abu Seer thought, feeling very sorry for them. *What in the world happened?*

Soon the admiral returned. He saw the dead bodies of the two cooks, with their heads lying a few feet away, and he saw the ring on Abu Seer's finger.

"Stop! Don't move your hand! The one with the ring on it! If you do, you'll kill me, too!"

"I won't make a move," said Abu Seer.

"Take it off, right now, and put it in your pocket!"

Abu Seer took off the ring.

"Ah, that's better," said the admiral, with a sigh. He guessed that Abu Seer had found the magic ring, which somehow had fallen off the king's finger and dropped into the sea.

"Take me to the king," Abu Seer said.

"Certainly," said the admiral. "You have nothing to be afraid of now. In fact, if you want to, you can kill the king and the whole army as well, and be king yourself. Just put on the ring and point at them."

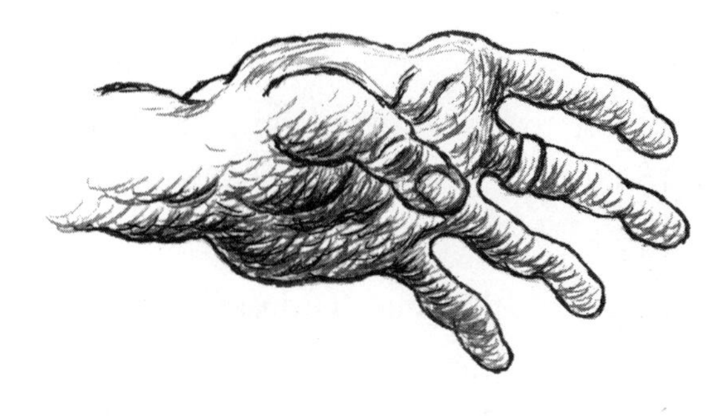

He took Abu Seer to the throne room. The king looked very anxious. His brow was furrowed, and he kept his hands hidden behind his back.

"My goodness," said the king. "Didn't we just throw you into the sea? How did you escape?"

Abu Seer told him the whole story: how the admiral had saved his life, how the fish had swallowed the ring, how *he* had cut open the fish and put on the ring and accidentally killed the two cooks, and how he was very sorry about that but he hadn't known what he was doing. "Anyway, Your Majesty," he said, handing over the ring, "I wanted to return this to you. You were always kind and generous to me, except for our last meeting, and I wanted to show you that I'm grateful. And if I have offended you in any way, please tell me. I have thought and thought about it, but I still can't understand why you were so angry at me."

As soon as the king put the ring back on his finger he felt much better. He walked up to Abu Seer and embraced him.

"Anyone but you would have kept the ring for himself," he said. "Thank you from the bottom of my heart."

"You're very welcome, Your Majesty," said Abu Seer. "But please, tell me what my crime was."

"Oh, I know now that you are innocent," the king said. "Only an innocent man would return this ring." And he repeated Abu Keer's accusations.

"That massage oil?" said Abu Seer. "But it's perfectly harmless. It may smell bad, but it feels wonderful. And, anyway, it was Abu Keer's idea to use it on you."

Then he told the king the whole story: how Abu Keer had sponged off him on the ship and in the hotel, how Abu Keer had taken his money and left him sick and helpless, and how Abu Keer had insulted and whipped him in the dye shop.

The king was furious. He had his guards arrest Abu Keer and bring him to the palace.

"You monster!" the king shouted. "I am going to have you stripped naked and whipped in front of your own shop. And I will personally rub that massage oil into your wounds, with a little salt and cayenne pepper sprinkled in. And then I am going to have your mouth sewn shut so that you can't tell any more lies. And then I'm going to have you stuffed inside a bag and dropped into the sea. How do you like *that*?"

"But this is absurd, Your Gracious Majesty," Abu Keer said. "It must all be a terrible misunderstanding."

"Misunderstanding, my eye!" said the king.

"Please, Your Majesty," Abu Seer said. "I have forgiven him so many times. I beg you to forgive him just this once."

"Of course I will forgive him," said the king. "*After* he's dead."

So the guards hauled Abu Keer away.

"Now, my friend," said the king, "ask me for anything you want."

"Well, Your Majesty," Abu Seer said, "what I'd really like is to go back to Alexandria. Not that I don't love it here in your beautiful city. But I'm a little homesick."

"Of course," said the king. "I understand."

And he gave Abu Seer a ship filled with gold and jewels and precious rugs and commanded its captain to take Abu Seer straight home.

Three weeks later, when they landed in Alexandria, they found a large bag washed up on the beach. Inside it was Abu Keer, dead. They buried him near the beach. Abu Seer had a gravestone carved for him that read:

HERE LIES ABU KEER.
AS A MASTER DYER, HE MADE NO MISTAKES.
AS A FRIEND, HE MADE MANY.
MAY GOD SHINE INTO HIS SOUL.

Aladdin and the Magic Lamp

CHAPTER 1

A VERY LONG time ago, in a city in China, there lived a poor tailor with his wife and his only son, who was named Aladdin.

Aladdin was a very brave, intelligent boy, but he was also headstrong and disobedient. His father wanted him to follow in

his footsteps and become a tailor. But Aladdin wasn't interested. "Someday I'm going to be rich and powerful," he would say. "And then I won't have to earn my living with a needle and thread. Just wait and see." His mother and father would shake their heads and tell him that he was a dreamer. "You won't be able to support yourself if you don't learn a trade. Be a good boy and forget these foolish thoughts." But Aladdin could never be convinced.

Instead of spending his days in his father's shop, he spent them in the streets with a gang of unruly boys. Aladdin was the ringleader. They would play games all day long: games with balls and sticks and stones, team games and games for two players, games of running and jumping and crawling and rolling and climbing, games in which you had to balance things on your head or your big toe or on the end of your nose, games in which you had to remember long lists of things or invent new names for the most everyday objects or insult your friends just enough to make them laugh and not get angry, games of hide-and-seek, games with pebbles as pieces that they played on an old chessboard someone had found leaning against the wall in an alley. Aladdin was usually the winner in these games, because he was smarter and faster than the rest of the boys.

When they got tired of the games, they would make up little dramas and act them out. Actually, it was Aladdin who would make up the dramas and assign all the roles. He would always assign the leading role to himself. He would be the king or the emperor, and the other boys would be his servants or his enemies.

When they got tired of the dramas, Aladdin would come up with a scheme for a great adventure that usually got them into trouble. He would dare someone to steal a peach from the grocer's stand (it had to be while the grocer was watching) and then to run around the block and put the peach back onto the peach pile before the grocer or his dog could catch up. Or he would lead them to some rich man's door, and they would all stand in front of it, singing and screaming at the top of their lungs, and when the rich man's butler opened the door, they would laugh and run away. One time they found a sheet of heavy gray paper and made a pair of ear flaps out of it, then stuck the flaps over the ears of the mayor's horse when no one was watching. The horse looked like a huge, long-nosed rabbit. They laughed so hard that they could barely remain standing.

Aladdin's parents were very disappointed in him. They called him a lazy, disobedient good-for-nothing. They were sure that he was going to end up as a beggar in the streets.

After his father died, his mother sold the tailor's shop and bought a spinning wheel. She made just enough money spinning yarn to eke out a living for herself and her son. There was barely enough to get by on, but she could almost always put a little food on the table when Aladdin came home. He showed up twice a day for meals. That was the only time he saw his mother. He was never rude to her; on the contrary, when he was with her, he was respectful and affectionate. But he never paid any attention to her constant nagging that he should get a job.

One day when Aladdin was ten, as he was playing with the other boys in the street right outside the candle maker's shop, a stranger walked by, stopped in front of them, and began staring at Aladdin. The stranger was a tall, dark-skinned man with a long nose; he was dressed in white robes, and on his head he wore a white turban.

This man was a powerful sorcerer who had come from the faraway land of Morocco. One day, six months before, during a magic ritual, he had seen an image of Aladdin's face in the center stone of his crystal necklace. He then learned that Aladdin was the only person who could hand over to him the most valuable

treasure in the world, a treasure he had been trying to locate for a dozen years. Now that he saw Aladdin, he smiled to himself. *Finally I've found the filthy little ragamuffin!* he thought. *All I have to do now is persuade him to come with me. That should be a piece of cake.*

The sorcerer walked into the shop and said to the candle maker, "Good afternoon."

"Good afternoon, sir," the candle maker said. "May I help you?"

"Yes," said the sorcerer, and he pointed through the open doorway to Aladdin and his friends. "Do you know those boys?"

The candle maker leaned over the counter and looked out the open door. "Of course," he said with a smile. "I know the little scoundrels well. They are always getting into trouble."

"Do you know the one in the middle?" the sorcerer asked.

"You mean Aladdin?" said the candle maker. "He's the biggest troublemaker of them all. But he's a very bright little fellow, and for all his mischief, he has a good heart."

"So Aladdin is his name," the sorcerer said. "And what is his father's name?"

"Oh," the candle maker said, "his father died three years ago, God rest his soul. His name was Ismail. He was a good tailor, a very hardworking man, but he never made much money. People say that he died of frustration over his good-for-nothing son. But *I* think that it was his weak heart that killed him."

"Thank you," said the sorcerer. "Here is something for your trouble," and he put a small copper coin on the counter.

"No trouble at all, sir," the candle maker said. "Many thanks."

The sorcerer left the shop and walked straight up to

Aladdin. He took the boy aside, and with tears in his eyes, he said, "Could it . . . Could it really be Aladdin? I can hardly believe this! It's too good to be true!"

"What's too good to be true, sir?" Aladdin said.

"Is your name Aladdin?"

"Yes."

"And are you the son of Ismail the tailor?"

"Yes, I am. But he died three years ago."

At these words the sorcerer threw his arms around Aladdin and burst into sobs.

When the sorcerer's sobbing stopped, Aladdin said, "Why are you crying, sir? Did you know my father?"

"Did I *know* him!" said the sorcerer. "I am his brother!"

"I didn't know he had a brother," Aladdin said.

"Well, of course you didn't," the sorcerer said. "We were parted when we were young men. I left for Morocco, which is a long, long way from here, and your father left for this town, and I made him promise never to mention me."

"Why did you do that, sir?"

"I was on a very dangerous mission, and I didn't want any of my enemies to know that your father was related to me. It would have been a death sentence for him."

"Really!" Aladdin said. "But you don't look at all like my father. Your skin is dark, your nose is very long, and your beard is bushy, while my father's skin was yellow and smooth and his nose was short, just like mine."

"Ah, you noticed," said the sorcerer. "You are very smart, just as smart as my dear brother was."

"That's strange, sir," Aladdin said. "No one ever said that my father was smart."

"Care and trouble may have clouded his mind," the sorcerer said. "But when he was young, he was as smart as anyone you'd ever meet. His mind was like lightning."

"But how is it that you don't look at all like him, sir?" Aladdin said.

"Ah yes, you asked me that before," said the sorcerer. "You are certainly a sharp-sighted young fellow. Well, the truth of the matter is that when I was a young man, I went to a great deal of trouble to disguise myself because of that dangerous mission. I had the best surgeons in the world operate on my face. They changed the color of my skin, made my whole face longer, even gave me a new nose, just so that I could protect myself and my dear brother. I had to pay them a lot of money, I assure you. After the operation, I had a new face and a new identity. That's when I moved to North Africa. But enough about me. Tell me about yourself. How is your dear mother?"

"Oh, she's all right," Aladdin said. "She works very hard. I don't see her very much."

"Well, I would like to present her with this gift, a small token of my brotherly love," the sorcerer said, taking out his purse. He counted three silver coins and put them into Aladdin's palm.

Aladdin was astonished. He had never touched so much money in his life. In fact, he had never even touched *one* silver coin.

"Take these to your dear mother," the sorcerer said, "with my compliments. Tell her that her husband's brother—your uncle—has returned after twenty years and that he will pay her a visit tomorrow morning."

Aladdin thanked the sorcerer and ran home as fast as he could.

"Mother! Mother!" he shouted as he dashed into the house. "My uncle has returned! I met him! He's back!"

"What's all this nonsense?" Aladdin's mother said. "You don't *have* an uncle. What kind of trick are you trying to play on me now?"

"No, this isn't a trick! I swear!" Aladdin said. "My uncle really has returned. We don't know about him because my father had to take an oath of secrecy because my uncle left on a dangerous mission and his enemies would have killed us if they had known that father was related to him and that's why we never knew."

"Nonsense!" said Aladdin's mother. "It's all a lie. Your father never told me about a brother, and that means he never *had* a brother."

"Oh, and he gave me these," Aladdin said, taking the three silver coins out of his pocket. They lay on his palm, shining.

"Dear God!" Aladdin's mother said. "Could it really be true?" And she burst into tears.

The next morning, for once, Aladdin stayed home. He and his mother sat down at the kitchen table and waited. They were too excited to say a word.

At nine o'clock they heard three loud raps. Aladdin's mother, her heart pounding, got up and opened the door. She was surprised to see a tall, dark-skinned man standing there, in white robes and a white turban.

"Good morning, dear lady," the sorcerer said. "May I come in?"

"Yes, sir," said Aladdin's mother, in a voice barely louder than a whisper. "Please come in. You are very welcome here, sir."

The sorcerer walked in, carrying a large bowl of fruit and a bottle of wine. After putting the fruit and wine on the rickety table, he began to sniffle. Tears rolled slowly down his cheeks.

"Why are you crying, sir?" Aladdin's mother asked.

"I'm thinking of my dear brother," the sorcerer said. "Please, for the love of God, show me where he used to sit."

"Over there, sir," Aladdin's mother said, pointing to a little rickety chair near the wall.

The sorcerer walked over to the chair, sank to his knees, and burst into loud tears. "Oh, my dear, dear brother!" he sobbed. "Light of my eyes! Comfort of my soul! Dearest, kindest brother that any man ever had! What a misfortune that you are dead! How wretched my whole existence is, now that I know I will never see you again! I wish to God I had died instead of you, my dear, dear brother! Oh, misery! Oh, sorrow! Oh, grief!"

"Please, sir," Aladdin's mother said, putting her hand on the sorcerer's shoulder, "please don't be so sad. You will hurt yourself."

"How can I stay alive when my poor dear brother is dead?" the sorcerer sobbed. "Life is not worth living without him." His sobs grew faster and louder, until finally he was pounding the floor with his fists. "I want to die!" he screamed. "I want to die!" As he said these words he pretended to faint.

"Quick, get some water!" Aladdin's mother said.

Aladdin ran to the water bucket, took a cupful, and splashed it on the sorcerer's face. The sorcerer immediately sat up, with a loud grunt. His face was dripping wet. He looked to the right, then to the left, up to the ceiling, then down to the floor. "Where am I?" he said.

"You're in the house of your brother," Aladdin's mother said.

"Ah, yes," said the sorcerer. He seemed much calmer now. "Did your son explain why you never heard a word about me?"

"Yes he did, sir. I must admit that when I first heard your story, I doubted it. But now that I see how brokenhearted you are, I believe you. You must have loved my husband very much."

"I loved him more than life itself," the sorcerer said. "But come to the table. Have some of the delicious fruit and wine that I brought you. I want to talk about my nephew. I want to do something for him."

"You do?" said Aladdin's mother as she bit into a large, luscious pear. It had been five years since she'd been able to afford a piece of fruit. The taste made her sigh with pleasure.

"Yes, indeed," said the sorcerer. "Now that my dear brother is gone—may God rest his soul—I stand in the place of a father to the boy. I want to do everything I can for him, and since, by the grace of God, I am a wealthy man, I can help him get ahead in the world very easily."

"That is wonderful, sir," Aladdin's mother said. "You are very kind. I couldn't dream of a finer brother-in-law."

"Yes, I will certainly make his career," the sorcerer said. "By the way, what *is* your career, young man?"

"I don't have one, sir," Aladdin said. "Not yet. But I know that whatever it is, I'll be a success."

"Oh, sir, don't pay any attention to his nonsense," said Aladdin's mother. "He is a lazy, mischievous, good-for-nothing little rascal who was never willing to learn a trade and drove his dear father into the . . ." Suddenly she realized that if she went on talking in this way, her brother-in-law might change his mind; he might think so badly of Aladdin that he wouldn't carry out his promise to help him. "Actually," she continued, "what I mean is that he's an unusual boy, not like your run-of-the-mill apprentices. He's a very creative child, you know. He has a golden tongue, and you can sit and listen to his stories for hours on end. His mind is quicker than any child's I ever met. I don't see him as much as I'd like to, but his father and I always agreed that he was the best son a parent could ever have."

"Really, Mother?" Aladdin said. "You never told me that before. It's awfully sweet of you to say."

"Not at all, dear child," said Aladdin's mother, blushing.

"Well, then," the sorcerer said, "since the boy doesn't have a regular career yet, I will set him up as a merchant. Would you enjoy that, my boy?"

"I don't know, sir," Aladdin said. "What would it be like?"

"First of all," said the sorcerer, "I will buy you four suits of the finest silk, and then I will take you to the public bath and have the attendants clean you from head to toe, rub you with fragrant oils, and dress you. You will come out looking like a prince and smelling like a rose. Then I will buy you a large booth at the bazaar, and I will fit it with the most elegant and desirable merchandise: cups and dishes of silver and gold, bolts of satin and silk, the highest-grade porcelain and crystal, scrolls painted on silk by the greatest artists in China—in short, only objects that the richest people in the land would want to have in their houses. And I will train you personally. I will teach you how to buy and sell. I'm sure that within a very short time, you will learn how to carry on the business by yourself, and you will become a very wealthy merchant, sought after and admired by all."

"I would like that," Aladdin said. "Thank you, sir."

"Oh, sir," said Aladdin's mother, "that is such a generous offer. How can we ever repay you?"

"There is no need to repay me, dear lady," the sorcerer said. "I am only doing my duty as an uncle and a brother-in-law." Then, turning to Aladdin, he said, "Come, my son, let's go out and look for some fine clothes for you, and then we'll go to the public bath."

Aladdin said good-bye to his mother and walked out the door with the sorcerer. He could hardly keep from jumping up and down for joy. *This is going to be the greatest adventure of my life,* he thought.

The sorcerer led Aladdin through the bustling streets of the city. The first shop they passed had a silk suit displayed in its window. It was royal blue, Aladdin's favorite color. Aladdin pointed and said, "Let's stop here, Uncle. Would you buy me that suit? I think I'd look very nice in it. Very businesslike."

"No, my boy," the sorcerer said. "I will buy you far more splendid clothing than that."

"Really?" Aladdin said. "How can anything be more beautiful?"

"Wait and see," said the sorcerer.

They walked down street after street until they came to the outskirts of the city. Aladdin had never been here before; he had only known the poor, ragged sections of town. Now he saw the mansions and palaces of the very rich, and he was so astonished by their beauty that he forgot all about shopping. These palaces were surrounded by pleasure gardens and parks, with trees and flowers of every color and variety. Many of them had

a huge lawn, with a stream running through it, and a pond in the middle, with families of ducks and geese swimming on the water or sitting on the grass beside it. Through the iron gates, Aladdin could see noblemen on horses, and elegantly dressed ladies drinking tea under pavilions of multicolored silk. Through one gate he saw a fountain spouting water high into the air, and from all four sides of the pool around it, water poured in through the mouths of four golden lions. Aladdin had never dreamed that people could live in such luxury.

After a while they left the palaces and pleasure gardens behind. The landscape slowly changed from lush to desolate. There were fewer and fewer trees, until the only green you could see was from the small scrubby bushes scattered across the dusty soil. Finally Aladdin turned to the sorcerer and said, "Where are we going, Uncle? We've left the city, and there's only desert here."

"Be patient, my boy," the sorcerer said. "I know the way."

"But, Uncle," Aladdin said, "I thought you were going to buy me four silk suits. We've left all the shops behind."

"Don't worry," said the sorcerer. "I will get you far more than pretty clothes."

"But this is the desert, Uncle. There's nothing here. Please, let's go back."

"Hold your tongue, you ignorant little urchin!" the sorcerer said. "I know what I'm doing. Just keep walking."

Aladdin was a little frightened by these harsh words, so he kept quiet for a while. But soon he became exhausted from all the walking, and he couldn't help saying, "I'm so tired, Uncle. Can't we rest now?"

"No, we can*not*, you little scum," the sorcerer said. "Keep walking, or you'll be very sorry you stopped."

"I'm sorry I made you angry," Aladdin said.

"You'll be even sorrier if you keep talking," said the sorcerer.

They walked for another hour. Then they stopped in a valley between two barren mountains. The sorcerer was smiling. "Here we are, my boy. This is the place. I know it is. I can feel it in my bones."

"What place, Uncle?"

"This is the place that will make me . . . I mean, that will make *both* of us the richest men in the world. That is, if you obey my commands to the letter. Will you promise to do that?"

"Yes, Uncle," said Aladdin. "Of course I will."

"Then the first thing I want you to do is to gather me a pile of dry twigs. Bring them here as fast as you can. And don't dawdle."

As weary as he was, Aladdin also felt fascinated by the sorcerer's words. *What will happen now?* he thought. *How is this going to make us the richest men in the world?*

After Aladdin had gathered a pile of dry twigs, the sorcerer set fire to it, then took something out of his breast pocket. It was a little silver box, in the shape of a triangle, with a goat's head embossed on the cover. He opened it, took a pinch of incense between his thumb and his index finger, sprinkled the incense on the fire, and muttered some words that Aladdin couldn't understand.

Immediately there was a loud burst of thunder, the earth quaked, and the ground in front of them split open. Only a few inches in front of their feet, where there had been solid ground, there was now a ditch five feet wide and five feet deep. Aladdin was so terrified that he started to run away. But at his first movement, the sorcerer caught him and hit him on the back of his head so hard that his teeth were almost knocked out.

When he had recovered a bit from the pain, Aladdin said, "Uncle, what did I do? Why did you hit me?"

"My dear child," said the sorcerer, with tears in his eyes, "I only hit you for your own good, and I assure you that it hurt me more than it hurt you. In fact, I am deeply pained that you could even think of running away and leaving your only uncle in the lurch. How could you do that to me? How could you abandon me? What have I done to deserve your distrust?"

"I'm sorry," Aladdin said. "I was frightened. I didn't mean to leave you. I'm really sorry."

"Well, I forgive you," the sorcerer said. "Now, let's get down to business. Look over into the ditch. What do you see?"

"A lot of dirt and rocks, Uncle."

"Look a little to the right of us. What do you see?"

"Oh," said Aladdin. "There's a slab of white stone."

"Yes," the sorcerer said. "It's marble. And what else?"

"Well, there's a large copper ring attached to it."

"Yes, my boy, my dear nephew, my favorite child, apple of my eye, joy of my heart. Beneath that marble slab, there is a treasure that only you can find for me, a treasure that will make all the kings of the earth seem like paupers. No one but you has the power to lift that slab. Can you do it?"

"I don't know, Uncle," Aladdin said. "I will certainly try. But I don't know if I'm strong enough. Maybe you can give me a hand."

"It is forbidden for anyone to help you," the sorcerer said. "You must do it by yourself. And while you are pulling at the ring, you must say your own name and the names of your father and grandfather. Once you utter these three names, the slab will feel very light."

"All right," said Aladdin. "If you say so." He climbed down into the ditch, walked to the marble slab, and pulled at the huge copper ring. Nothing budged. Then he closed his eyes, whispered his name, his father's, and his grandfather's, and gave a yank. The marble slab lifted as easily as if it were made of paper. *Wow!* Aladdin thought. *My uncle was right: it* was *easy!*

In front of him was a marble staircase with twelve steps that

led down into a dark cave. "What should I do now?" he said, looking up at the sorcerer.

"Do exactly as I tell you," the sorcerer said. "If you don't follow every detail of my instructions, you will ruin this whole adventure, and you may even cause your own death."

This is serious, Aladdin thought. *I'd better listen very carefully.*

"First of all," said the sorcerer, "walk down the steps. At the bottom you'll find a large cave that is divided into four rooms. In each of these rooms, you'll see a large brass urn filled with silver and gold. Do not touch these urns! Don't even let your clothes brush against them! If you even brush against them with the hem of your sleeve, you'll be turned into a black stone, and that will be the end of you. Walk around each of these four urns, keeping at least a five-foot distance between you and them, until you have walked through all four rooms. At the back of the fourth room you will find a door. Open this door. It will lead you into a garden filled with fruit trees. Take the path through the fruit trees. It's about fifty yards long. Are you paying attention?"

"Yes, Uncle, I am."

"Good. The path leads to another room with a ladder in the middle. Climb the ladder and reach up and take down the lamp that is hanging there from the ceiling. Pour out the liquid and put the lamp into your largest pocket. Don't be afraid that the liquid will stain your clothes—it isn't oil, and as soon as you pour it out, the lamp will be dry. After you climb back down the ladder, you may pick any fruit you want from the trees. They belong to you, as long as you have the lamp."

"Yes, Uncle. I understand."

"One last thing," the sorcerer said. "Come here, to this side of the ditch." When Aladdin came, the sorcerer leaned over, took a ring from the middle finger of his right hand, and gave it to Aladdin. "This ring will protect you from almost any harm that can come to you. Put it on."

"Oh," said Aladdin, slipping on the ring. "Thank you."

"But it can only protect you if you follow my instructions to the letter. Will you do that?"

"I promise," Aladdin said. And he turned around, walked back to the marble staircase, and descended the stairs into the dark.

CHAPTER 4

Everything in the cave was just the way the sorcerer had said it would be. Aladdin walked very carefully around each of the four urns. In the fourth room, he opened the door into the garden, walked down the path through the fruit trees, came to the room with the ladder, climbed the ladder, took down the lamp, poured out the liquid, and put the lamp into his largest pocket. Then he climbed down the ladder and walked back on the path into the garden.

The garden seemed different, now that his task had been accomplished. He could take it in now, and he saw for the first time how very beautiful it was. When he looked at the branches of the fruit trees, he could see many kinds of birds, and he could hear them singing their hearts out. The chorus of birds sounded like a chorus of children's voices, and he was so moved by their songs that he thought he could almost understand what they were saying.

As Aladdin looked at the branches he became aware that they were covered not with fruit but with sparkling jewels: diamonds, emeralds, sapphires, pearls, rubies, and many other kinds of precious stones. Some of them were as big as oranges, some even bigger than grapefruits; the smallest of them were of a size that dwarfed even the most splendid gems owned by the richest monarchs in the world. Since Aladdin was a poor boy and had no experience of jewels, he thought that they must be made of glass. But they were very beautiful, and he decided to take them home to add to his collection of rocks and pebbles, which he kept hidden under a loose board in his bedroom. So he filled his pockets with jewels. After his pockets were full, he stuffed more jewels under his belt and inside his shirt and socks, until his clothes were bulging with precious stones. With every step he took, he could hear the *click, click* of jewels tapping against each other.

Finally he arrived at the staircase that led out of the cave. Step by step, with difficulty—all the jewels that he'd stuffed into his clothing were weighing him down—he ascended the staircase. When he reached the final step, which was higher than the rest, he called up to the sorcerer, "Lend me a hand, Uncle. I don't think I can make it by myself."

"First give me the lamp, my boy," the sorcerer said. "Then I'll help you up."

"No, no, Uncle," Aladdin said. "It's not the lamp that's weighing me down. Just lend me a hand. I'll give you the lamp as soon as I'm out of here."

"Don't be stubborn, boy. Give me the lamp!"

"But, Uncle, it's buried under—"

"I don't care where it is, you little scoundrel. Give me the lamp right now! Do you hear me? Right now!"

"But, Uncle—"

"Don't you 'But, Uncle' me! Hand over that lamp, you filthy little beggar! Hand it over right now if you know what's good for you!"

"I can't," said Aladdin. "Just listen to me for a moment. The reason I can't is . . ."

But the sorcerer was so consumed by rage that it was as if his ears were stopped up with wax. He couldn't hear what Aladdin was saying. His fear and greed could only see fear and greed in

Aladdin, and he thought Aladdin was trying to steal the lamp from him. He was so furious about Aladdin's treachery that he ran over to the fire, threw more incense onto it, and uttered some magic words. Immediately the earth quaked, there was a loud thunderclap, and once again the marble slab sealed the entrance to the cave.

"God curse you!" the sorcerer shouted into the ditch. "I was so close to my heart's desire! And now you have ruined it forever, you miserable little wretch. You can die here in this dark cave, never knowing what a treasure you possess. And may it be a slow, agonizing death." Then he stamped off, shouting and cursing, and headed back to Morocco.

After a dozen steps he turned around and shouted toward the ditch, "Oh, and when you begin to die of starvation, my boy, remember that there's plenty of fruit on the trees."

CHAPTER 5

For an hour Aladdin screamed, begged, and pleaded for help. Finally he gave up and sat down on the steps, crying.

He was in total darkness. He didn't know what to do. He couldn't think of anything *to* do. He was frightened, but not too frightened, because he knew that there was nothing dangerous in the cave. He was aware that he might starve to death, but perhaps there was something to eat in the garden, if only he could find his way there with his hands instead of with his eyes. For the time being, he thought, the best course of action was to stay put.

How could his uncle have buried him alive like this? How could a man do such a mean thing to his own nephew? To react with such rage just because Aladdin couldn't follow his orders right away: it wasn't natural. It wasn't what an uncle would do. *Hmmm*, he thought. *There's something awfully strange here.*

Aladdin began to review the facts. It was clear that his uncle (if he *was* his uncle) didn't love him—didn't even care about him. It was also very clear that he was a sorcerer and had some impressive magical powers. And, obviously, the only thing he wanted was the treasure. Then there was the fact that he didn't look at all like Aladdin's father. And his whole story about the dangerous mission, now that Aladdin remembered it, could easily have been a pack of lies.

The more Aladdin thought about the sorcerer, the more suspicious he became. Finally, he came to the conclusion that the man couldn't have been his uncle, and that whoever he was, he was not a kind man.

Aladdin was so tired by now that he fell asleep on the steps. He woke up hours later, cold and very hungry. He felt his way, in the pitch dark, down the steps to the first room. He flattened himself against the wall, so that he could be sure not to get anywhere near the golden urns. When he arrived at the fourth room, he slowly moved to the garden door. The door was locked. Aladdin shook the handle with all his might, but it wouldn't budge. All he could do now was feel his way back to the steps.

He was really frightened now. He was cold, he was hungry, there was no food, no light, no way of getting out, no one who could help him.

He slept and woke, then slept again. Hours passed, days passed. He completely lost track of time.

Finally, in despair, he put his palms together and began to pray. "Dear God," he said, "please help me. I know I haven't always been a good boy, but . . ."

As he said these last words his right hand happened to make a tiny movement, so that his fingers, ever so gently, rubbed against the sorcerer's ring on the middle finger of his left hand. All at once there was a flash of light, a sound like a thunderclap, and there before his eyes stood an enormous genie. The genie was ten feet tall and very muscular. He was wearing a vest of crimson velvet and royal-blue silk pants. He looked very fierce, and with his thick golden hair, thick golden eyebrows, and bushy golden beard, he seemed rather like a lion, if a lion had been transformed into a very tall man.

"O Master, your wish is my command," the genie bellowed. "Ask me for anything your heart desires, and I shall make it happen. For I am the slave of whoever wears the blessed ring."

At first Aladdin was frightened, then he was astonished, then he was absolutely delighted. "Genie," he said, "take me out of this cave and put me back on the ground."

No sooner had he issued the command than he found himself standing outside the cave. He had been in the dark so long that the sunlight hurt his eyes, and he had to cover them for a few minutes with his hands. When he was finally able to look, he recognized that he was on the very same patch of ground from which he had descended into the cave. Only now there was no ditch, no marble slab, and no copper ring. The earth was completely level, without a trace of an entrance. Over to the left were the charred remains of the twigs he had gathered for the fire.

He looked around for the genie, but saw no one. He wanted to go home quickly, because he was very tired and hungry, and

for a moment he considered rubbing the ring again and commanding the genie to take him home. But on second thought, he decided to walk home. After all, there might be a limited number of commands that the genie would obey, and he didn't want to waste one on something he could do for himself.

When Aladdin got home, he was so weak and hungry that he fainted as soon as he walked in. His mother revived him, fed him, and put him to bed. He slept uninterruptedly for a day and a half.

When he finally woke up, his mother asked him where he had been, what he had done, and where his dear uncle was. Aladdin told her everything that had happened to him and ended with his conclusions about his so-called uncle.

"It was too good to be true," his mother said, crying. "It's not for the likes of us to be dreaming about silk clothes and merchants' shops. Poor you were, and poor you will always be."

"But, Mother," Aladdin said, "at least we have the silver coins the imposter gave us. We're better off than we were before."

"It was too good to be true," his mother repeated. "And as I always said, you will end up a beggar in the streets."

Chapter 6

That afternoon Aladdin took all the pretty stones he had come home with and put them under the loose board in his bedroom with the rest of his rocks and pebbles. The lamp he put by the side of his bed.

Because of the three silver coins, Aladdin's mother worked much less than before. After all the coins had been spent, though, Aladdin's mother came to him and said, "I haven't needed to work for a while. But all our money is gone now. So I will have to go back to the spinning wheel."

"Wait, Mother," Aladdin said. "I have a better idea. You know that old lamp I brought back from the cave? I'm sure it's worth *some*thing. I'll go to the market and sell it, and we can live off that money for a while."

"All right," Aladdin's mother said. "But let me clean it first. It's filthy, and it will sell for a higher price if I polish it."

"Good idea," Aladdin said. He hurried to his room, picked

up the lamp, ran back, and handed it to his mother, who began rubbing the dirt off it.

All at once there was a flash of light, a sound like the crashing of cymbals, and there before their eyes stood an enormous genie. Aladdin's mother fainted.

The genie was twenty feet tall and very muscular. He was wearing a vest of royal-blue velvet and royal-blue silk pants. He had a fierce expression on his face, thick red hair, thick red eyebrows, and a bushy red beard.

"O Master, your wish is my command," the genie roared. "Ask me for anything your heart desires, and I shall make it happen. For I am the slave of whoever owns the blessed lamp."

Aladdin was not at all frightened. He had been through this before. "Genie," he said, "my mother and I are hungry. Bring us something to eat, and let it be something delicious. Please."

"Yes, Master," the genie said, then vanished. A split second later he reappeared with a huge silver tray the size of the kitchen table. On the tray there were twelve silver plates, each one piled high with the most exquisite food Aladdin had ever seen or smelled: roast beef, filet mignon, barbecued chicken, lamb chops, charbroiled fish, and sumptuous vegetable dishes, all of them prepared in a variety of ways according to recipes that the greatest chefs in the world would have envied. There were also ten loaves of bread, each one made from a different grain; pitchers of juice, tea, and coffee; five flasks of vintage wine; and thirteen different desserts, ranging from the most luscious, flakiest-looking cherry and apple pies to gigantic chocolate-chip cookies to cheesecake and chocolate cake to crystal bowls filled with pistachio, almond, cherry-chocolate, and mocha-chip ice cream.

Aladdin had never even dreamed of this kind of food. His eyes bulged. His mouth watered. He was about to help himself when he remembered that his mother was still stretched out on the floor. He put a little water on her forehead and woke her up. "Mother," he said. "Get up! Look what we have for dinner!"

Aladdin's mother took one look at the splendid meal and fainted again.

When Aladdin woke her a second time, she said, "Dear God! Where did all this luxury come from? Is this real? Am I dreaming?"

"No, Mother," Aladdin said. "It's all real. I'll explain it later. Let's eat."

After they had eaten to their hearts' content (and their stomachs' content as well), Aladdin told his mother about the genie of the ring and the genie of the magic lamp and how they had promised to do whatever he commanded.

"I'm frightened of these genies," Aladdin's mother said. "I don't want to have anything to do with them. Poor folks like us shouldn't deal with this kind of power, anyway. It's not proper. Please, I beg of you, throw away the lamp and the ring. They're dangerous and will only cause you grief."

"I see how frightened you are, Mother," Aladdin said. "But the ring and the lamp are gifts from God, and I wouldn't feel right about throwing them away. I know that I can use them wisely. Don't worry. I promise you, you won't ever have to deal with a genie in the future. I will take care of that myself."

"Well," said Aladdin's mother, "the lamp and the ring belong to you—you're the one who has to decide. Just don't ever bring that big, horrible red monster into my kitchen again."

In two days the food was gone. Aladdin wrapped one of the silver plates in a cloth, went to the bazaar, and asked around until he found a goldsmith's shop. He walked in, took out the plate, and said, "I would like to sell this, sir. How much is it worth?"

The goldsmith looked at the plate admiringly, weighed it, and said, "This is pure silver, young man. I haven't seen such fine merchandise in a very long time. I will give you seventy-two gold pieces for it."

"Really?" Aladdin said. "That's wonderful. Thank you, sir."

"How did you come upon such extraordinarily beautiful merchandise?" the goldsmith asked.

"It was a gift, sir," Aladdin said, "from a very tall friend of mine."

"Well, young man," said the goldsmith, "if your friend ever gives you more gifts of this sort, bring them to me, and I will always be glad to pay you a fair price for them."

That is precisely what Aladdin continued to do. Every time the money was gone, he would bring in another plate, and the merchant would buy it. After all twelve plates had been sold, Aladdin brought in the huge silver tray. And after the silver tray had been sold, Aladdin would take out the magic lamp, rub it, and command the genie to bring him a whole new meal. (He would always make sure that his mother was out of the house when he did this.) After the food had been eaten, he would start selling the plates again.

A dozen years passed in this way. Aladdin was now twenty-two years old. He and his mother were no longer poor. They always had more than enough money now to live a comfortable life, though they lived quite modestly and didn't even move out of their poor neighborhood. The neighbors were aware that Aladdin's mother no longer had to spin yarn. But no one knew how she earned her living. There were rumors about a wealthy uncle or wealthy friends. But when people asked Aladdin, he would just smile and say, "Friends are such a blessing, aren't they?"

During these years Aladdin's habits changed. He began to spend more and more time in the bazaar. He was no less playful and creative, and he still loved games and dramas and hijinks, but he took a great deal of interest now in business as well. He learned much from the goldsmith and through him was introduced to some of the most prominent jewelers and merchants in the city. Some of them became his friends and mentors, and he was grateful for their teaching. Over the years he learned not only how to buy and sell, but also how to appreciate the beauty of the merchandise that he saw—the cups and dishes of silver and gold, the satins and silks, the porcelain and crystal, the jewels, the sculptures and paintings. He also quickly became aware that the stones he had brought back from the cave weren't made of glass at all, but were extremely rare and precious gems, and that even the largest diamonds, emeralds, sapphires, rubies, and pearls that the jewelry merchants sold to the king were half the size of the smallest of the jewels he had brought home.

Aladdin was now well known and well respected among the merchants of the city but was still living a very modest life in his old neighborhood. He hadn't needed to call on either genie for years, because he was making a great deal of money as a merchant. Life was good, and he was very satisfied with it.

One day, as Aladdin was walking to the bazaar, the town crier began to call out, "Make way for Princess Laila! Make way for the princess!" Immediately everyone hurried to either side of the broad street. They stood there, tightly packed, like a crowd waiting for a parade to pass. People pushed and shoved to have a better view. Women asked other women to please shut their parasols. Fathers took their little children and lifted them up onto their shoulders.

Soon the princess arrived, attended by her ladies and her slaves. The court ladies were wearing magnificent gowns of blue and green and red and yellow, with designs of flowers or birds or trees on them, and headdresses and necklaces studded with precious stones. But the princess was dressed very simply, in a cream-colored silk dress, and the only jewelry she wore was a pair of pearl earrings. As she walked down the street she seemed not to notice the cheering of the crowd, or its oohs and ahhs. She seemed to be completely absorbed in her inner world, and there was a small, peaceful smile on her lips.

Aladdin had never seen anyone or anything so beautiful as the princess. He felt his heart opening to her, the way a flower opens in the sunlight. Even though he had just seen her for the first time, it was as if he knew her better than anyone he had ever met—as if she were his best friend and they had known each other a long, long time ago and he had just recognized her again after all that time. From the first instant he saw her face, he knew that his life would never be the same.

After the princess and her attendants had gone and the crowd had dispersed, Aladdin walked home. He was so deeply absorbed in his feelings about the princess that he looked like a sleepwalker as he entered his house. His mother spoke to him several times, but he didn't hear her. Finally she had to shout, "Aladdin! Aladdin! What's the matter with you? Are you sick?"

Aladdin shook his head. "No, I'm fine, Mother. I can't talk to you now. But I'm perfectly all right."

"Why can't you talk to me? Tell me how you are. Please. I'm worried about you."

"Don't worry, Mother. I just need to be silent right now. I'll tell you all about it this evening at dinner, when I've had a chance to let this sink in."

"To let *what* sink in?"

"I'll tell you all about it," Aladdin repeated.

His mother was burning with curiosity, but she left him alone.

By dinnertime Aladdin was ready to talk. "Mother," he said, "I have fallen in love."

"Oh, so that's why you look that way," his mother said, smiling. "That's wonderful. Who is she?"

"She's the most beautiful girl you can imagine," Aladdin said.

"Does she come from a good family?" Aladdin's mother asked. "I hope she does. I don't want you to marry into a family of riffraff."

"Yes, Mother," Aladdin said. "She comes from a very good family. Her name is Laila. Her father is His Majesty the king."

"*Princess* Laila?" Aladdin's mother said. "Are you out of your mind? Have you gone stark raving mad?"

"No, Mother," Aladdin said. "It's just that I'm in love. The princess is my heart's desire, and I won't rest until I have married her."

"My poor child," Aladdin's mother said, "be reasonable, I beg you. There's no way in the world that you could marry the king's daughter. Even if she were to love you, the king would never let her marry a commoner. He would never even let her marry a nobleman. In fact, he wouldn't let her marry anyone but a king who was equal to him in rank and wealth. It's not a possibility. Surely you can recognize that."

"I recognize nothing of the sort, Mother," Aladdin said. "I know that she will marry me and that the king will be happy to have me as a son-in-law."

"My poor boy, you've gone completely crazy. You've become just as foolish a dreamer as you used to be when you were a child. How can the king possibly accept you? Your father was a poor tailor, and his father was poor before him, and his father's father as well. And my family was no better. We had to struggle all our lives just to keep food on the table and not sink to the level of the beggars in the street. Please, I implore you, give up this insane fantasy. There are lots of pretty girls who would be only too happy to marry a rich young man like you."

"Mother, Princess Laila is the girl I'm in love with, and Princess Laila is the girl I'm going to marry."

"But, Aladdin, how can you do that? She doesn't know you exist. How can you get to see the king to ask for her hand in marriage? It takes even important people years before they can arrange a meeting with him. There's a waiting list of thousands!"

"I have a plan," Aladdin said. "As a matter of fact, my plan involves *you*."

"Me? What can I have to do with this madness?"

"Well, Mother, I would like you to go to court and ask the king, on my behalf, for the hand of his daughter in marriage."

"Oh, son," said Aladdin's mother, "you are making no sense at all. How is such a plan possible? Even if I could get to speak with the king—even if I could manage to make such an outrageous request—the king would think I was a madwoman. 'Your Majesty: my son, the son of Ismail the tailor, asks for Princess Laila's hand in marriage.' They would put me in chains and haul me off to the asylum. They might even cut off my head."

"It doesn't make any sense to you now," Aladdin said. "But

trust me. The jewels that I brought home from the cave are beyond price. There's not a king in the world who can match even the smallest of them, and not a king in the world who wouldn't accept their owner as his son-in-law. Let's take some of them now and arrange them in our best porcelain bowl as a present for the king."

Shaking her head, Aladdin's mother brought the bowl to the kitchen table. Meanwhile, Aladdin pulled up the loose board in his bedroom, took out a dozen jewels, and brought them to the kitchen—a diamond and an emerald bigger than grapefruits, and three rubies, two emeralds, two sapphires, two pearls, and a diamond that were all as big as oranges. He arranged them in a pyramid, with the brightest gems on top.

"They certainly are splendid," Aladdin's mother said. "This is a present truly fit for a king."

"And I promise you, Mother, that the king will be delighted. Just make my request as you give him the jewels. And don't worry. Everything will be fine."

Early the next morning Aladdin's mother went to the palace, carrying the bowl of jewels wrapped in a large cloth. She went straight to the assembly hall and found a seat in the back row. Then she waited as the noblemen and ministers of state filed in, followed by a large crowd of merchants, lawyers, foreigners, people holding petitions, people holding babies, wealthy people dressed in gorgeous robes, and poor people dressed in threadbare clothes. It seemed as if everyone wanted something from the king.

Finally the king entered the room from another door. The audience stood up and waited, with their arms crossed over their chests. After the king had sat down on his throne, he motioned for all to be seated. They took their places according to rank, with the wealthiest and most powerful in the front rows. Then, one by one, people stood and read their petitions to the king, and he decided each case according to its merits. Things

proceeded in this way until noon, when a court official hit a large brass gong, signaling that the session was over for the day.

Aladdin's mother went to the palace every day. Every day she sat in the back row, waited until the end of the session, and returned home carrying the bowl of jewels. "Be patient, Mother," Aladdin would tell her. "Sooner or later you'll have an opportunity to speak with the king. I don't know how it will happen, but it will."

Eventually the king began to notice her. After a month, he turned to his prime minister and said, "Have you noticed a woman in the back row? She has been coming to the assembly hall every single day for weeks now."

"What woman, Your Majesty?" the prime minister said. "I haven't seen anyone in the back row but the usual riffraff."

"No," said the king, "this is quite an unusual woman. She doesn't talk, and she doesn't fidget. She seems very determined."

"Well, Your Majesty," the prime minister said, "she's probably determined to make a complaint about her husband or determined to prove that her neighbor stole an egg from under her favorite hen. You know how ridiculously petty these commoners can be."

"And every day she comes carrying something wrapped in a cloth," the king said. "I keep wondering what it could be. It's quite large. It looks rather heavy."

"Oh, Your Majesty," the prime minister said, "it's probably a couple of bricks that her husband threw at her. The woman is going to prove it by bringing the evidence."

"That woman interests me," said the king. "Bring her to me if she comes to the next session."

"Yes, of course, Your Majesty," the prime minister said, bowing deeply. "Your wish is my command."

The next morning the prime minister called for Aladdin's mother to be brought forward to the throne. She bowed, bent over, put the bowl on the floor, and bowed again. "All blessings to Your Majesty," she said. "I wish you health, happiness, peace throughout your kingdom, prosperity, and a long life."

"Yes, yes," said the king. "But tell me, why is it that you're here? I have seen you every day for the last several weeks. What is it that you wish from me?"

Aladdin's mother began to tremble. "Your Majesty," she said, "I do have a request. But I am frightened that it will offend you."

"Oh, fiddlesticks!" the prime minister said. "Have no fear, my good woman. Don't you know that His Majesty is known far and wide—throughout the civilized world, in fact—for his extraordinary kindness and mercy? State your request, and His Majesty will answer you as he sees fit."

"Well, Your Majesty," said Aladdin's mother to the king, "I have a son, a dear boy named Aladdin, who has fallen in love with your daughter, the beautiful princess Laila—may God bless and keep her—and my son requests the princess's hand in marriage."

"This is an outrage!" the prime minister shouted. "Shall I call the guards, Your Majesty? The woman is obviously insane."

Aladdin's mother waited for him to finish, then said, "And my son would like to give you a small present, Your Majesty, as a token of his loyalty and appreciation."

"A present?" said the king. "What kind of present?"

"This, Your Majesty," Aladdin's mother said, picking up the bowl and handing it to the king.

As the king removed the cloth his jaw dropped and his eyes bulged. Never had he seen such a dazzling collection of jewels. Never had he even imagined that jewels could be so immense, so brilliant, so beautiful as the jewels in this porcelain bowl. One by one he picked them up and examined them.

"My goodness gracious!" he finally said to the prime minister. "Have you ever seen anything so glorious? These make the jewels in my treasury seem absolutely puny. What do you think? Have you ever seen jewels as glorious as these?"

"Never, Your Majesty," the prime minister said.

"Well," said the king, "whoever can give such a magnificent present as this certainly deserves to become my son-in-law."

"But, Your Majesty," the prime minister said, whispering into the king's ear, "this woman is a commoner. Look at the way she's dressed; listen to the way she speaks."

"What does your husband do, my good woman?" the king asked.

"He is dead these many years, Your Majesty," Aladdin's mother said. "He was a tailor."

"You see, Your Majesty?" the prime minister whispered. "She's not only a commoner, but she comes from the lower classes. How can you allow such a low person as the son of a tailor to marry Princess Laila? It would be shameful. It would be beneath your dignity."

"On the other hand," the king said, whispering into the prime minister's ear, "her son is a most extraordinarily wealthy man. How else could he be the owner of such rare jewels? However humble his origins, he seems to be a man who could buy and sell me a thousand times over. It would be a very prudent thing to ally myself to such a man, don't you think?"

"At least have her wait, Your Majesty," the prime minister whispered. "Tell her to wait while you prepare for the wedding."

"All right," said the king. Then, turning to Aladdin's mother, he said, "Tell your son that I accept his request and that I thank him for the jewels. He may marry my daughter in three months' time. Once the wedding preparations are completed, he may come to the palace to claim her hand in marriage."

Aladdin's mother thanked the king and hurried home, smiling.

CHAPTER 10

Exactly three months later Aladdin's mother appeared at the palace. "Your Majesty," she said to the king, "three months have gone by, and now it's time to fulfill your promise."

"My promise?" said the king. "What promise?"

"Surely, Your Majesty, you remember that you promised your daughter to my son, Aladdin. You told me that once the wedding preparations were completed, he could claim her hand in marriage."

"Ah, yes," said the king. "But be patient, my good woman. Just wait a few more minutes, while I discuss the matter."

He turned to the prime minister and said, "What should I do? I did give her my word. And one's word is one's reputation. In this, kings are just like everyone else."

"That's true, Your Majesty," the prime minister said. "But how can you marry the princess to the son of a commoner like this? Look how plainly she is dressed. These people are unworthy of being taken into the family of your lowest servant, much less into your own family."

"But aren't you forgetting his gift?" the king said. "It was a magnificent gift."

"And you get to keep it, Your Majesty. It's yours, and you owe him nothing in return, because you are the king."

"Still," the king said, "I don't feel right about promising him my daughter and then breaking my word. Isn't there some other way?"

"Of course there is," said the prime minister. "Just tell this beggar that her son can have Princess Laila if he pays the marriage price for her, and then make the price so high that he can't possibly pay it."

"That's a fine idea," said the king. Then, turning to Aladdin's mother, he said, "My good woman, I have finished my consultation. And you are quite right: the three months have passed, and it's time for your son to marry my daughter. But there is one small detail that needs to be taken care of first."

"What detail is that?" asked Aladdin's mother.

"The matter of the marriage price," the king said.

"The marriage price?" Aladdin's mother said.

"Yes," said the king. "As the princess's marriage price, your son must provide me with forty large bowls of pure gold, filled to the brim with jewels like the ones you brought me. Each bowl must be carried by a slave and preceded by a slave girl. If your son can pay this marriage price, I will happily give him my daughter."

Aladdin's mother went home with a heavy heart. "All is

lost," she said to Aladdin. "I knew the king would never let people like us marry his daughter. It was a foolish dream from the beginning."

"What happened?" Aladdin asked.

When his mother told him, he laughed. "Is that all? I don't see a problem in the king's demand. Actually, I thought he would ask for a lot more."

"A lot more?" Aladdin's mother said. "He asked for more than anyone could bring him. He might as well have said, 'Bring me the moon.' You'll never be able to pay the marriage price. Why don't you just give up your fantasy, and marry some nice girl from a merchant family?"

"Now, Mother," Aladdin said. "Don't you worry. How about going out to the market now and getting us something good for dinner? I want the house to myself."

After she went out, Aladdin got the lamp from his room and rubbed it. All at once there was a flash of light, a sound like a long chord played by a hundred violins, and there before his eyes stood the genie of the lamp, in his vest of royal-blue velvet and his royal-blue silk pants. "O Master," the genie said, "your wish is my command. Ask me for anything your heart desires, and I shall make it happen. For I am the slave of whoever owns the blessed lamp."

"Hello," Aladdin said. "It's nice to see you again, after all these years."

The genie bowed.

"I have a job for you," Aladdin said. "Here is what I need: Bring me forty large bowls of pure gold, filled to the brim with fruits from the garden where I found your lamp. And also bring me forty slaves to carry the bowls and forty slave girls to walk in front of them."

"Yes, Master," the genie said, then vanished. A split second later he reappeared with the bowls, the slaves, and the slave girls. "O Master," he said, "here is what you desired. Is there anything else?"

"Not now," Aladdin said. "If there's something else, I'll call on you."

When Aladdin's mother returned from the market, she was astonished at the golden bowls, the slaves, and the slave girls. They filled her small house and spilled out into the small yard

behind it. When she took off the silver cloths embroidered with golden flowers that covered the bowls, she could see that each one was brimming with diamonds, pearls, emeralds, rubies, sapphires, and other precious stones even larger than the ones Aladdin had sent to the king.

"Mother," Aladdin said, "please go right back to the palace and present all this to the king, with my compliments." Then he commanded the forty slaves to pick up the forty golden bowls and to carry them, on their heads, out the door. Each slave was to be preceded by a slave girl, as the king had required.

As the slaves and slave girls issued into the street, the neighbors began to gather around. Soon there was a large crowd. People could hardly believe their eyes, so brilliant was the spectacle. The slaves and slave girls were all gorgeous; they had perfect features and perfectly formed bodies, and each one was beautiful in a different way. They were dressed in multicolored silk robes lined with cloth of gold and studded with diamonds, rubies, and emeralds, and their turbans were hung with strings of the most exquisite pearls. As they walked through the streets to the palace, they moved in perfect symmetry, like dancers.

When the first of the slaves reached the palace gates, the captain of the guards bowed deeply. "Welcome, Your Majesty," he said, thinking that some unknown king had arrived on a visit of state.

"You are mistaken, sir," the slave said. "We are only slaves. Our master will come later."

As the procession filed into the palace, the noblemen and ministers gathered to stare, just as Aladdin's neighbors had.

Although they all came from rich and powerful families, they had never seen such a display of magnificence as this. They were dazzled by the beauty of the slaves and slave girls, and many of the young men fell in love and wanted to propose on the spot.

Soon they were ushered into the assembly hall, where the king was still in council. Aladdin's mother bowed and said, "Your Majesty, here is the princess's marriage price. My son says that he is honored to present you with what you requested, and that the princess is worth a million times more than this."

After she had finished, the forty slaves put down the golden bowls, and the forty slave girls took off the cloths that covered the bowls.

The king was dumbstruck. He was so astonished by the beauty of the slave girls, the majesty of the slaves, and the size and brilliance of the jewels that he was unable to speak for five minutes. Finally he turned to the prime minister and said, "Well, what do you think now? Is such a man worthy enough to marry my daughter?"

The prime minister bowed and was silent.

"Tell your son," the king said to Aladdin's mother, "that he may claim my daughter this very night. Tonight he and Princess Laila will be married."

After Aladdin's mother left, the king led the procession to the princess's chambers. Princess Laila was as dazzled by the magnificence of Aladdin's present as the king had been. *What kind of man am I marrying?* she thought. *Certainly he is wealthy and generous beyond imagination. I hope that he is kind as well.*

Aladdin was overjoyed to hear the news. "Thank you so much for being my messenger, Mother," he said. "You did a wonderful job. Now if you would go out of the house one more time, for just a few minutes, I would really appreciate it."

"All right," said Aladdin's mother. "But make sure you don't call up that monster till I've shut the door."

After she went out, Aladdin got the lamp from his room and rubbed it. All at once, there was a flash of light, a sound like the singing of birds on a spring morning, and there before his eyes stood the genie of the lamp, in his vest of royal-blue velvet and his royal-blue silk pants. "O Master," the genie said, "your wish is my command. Ask me for anything your heart desires, and I shall make it happen. For I am the slave of whoever owns the blessed lamp."

"I have another job for you," Aladdin said. "First, dress me in the most glorious clothes ever worn by a human being."

"Done!" said the genie.

Aladdin looked down at his body. He was wearing a cream-colored silk robe of a quality that made all the silk he had ever seen or touched seem inferior, as artificial roses seem after you have touched a real rose. The robe was covered with diamonds and pearls, and was a thousand times more splendid than the slaves' robes that the crowds had been admiring.

"Is there anything else that you desire, Master?" asked the genie.

"Yes," Aladdin said. "Bring me a stallion stronger and swifter than any king has ever owned, and let its saddle and bridle be studded with the finest jewels. And I want twenty slaves to walk before me, all dressed as magnificently as the slaves who brought the jewels to the king, and twenty slaves to walk behind me. I also want you to dress my mother in clothing fit for a queen, bring her a fine mare to ride on, and I want six slave girls to accompany her. And I also want ten thousand gold coins, in ten separate purses."

"Is that all, Master?" the genie said.

"No," said Aladdin. "There's one more thing. I want you to make me the handsomest man in the world. Don't change my features or make me appear to be someone else. I still want to look like myself. But make me so handsome that Princess Laila can't help falling in love with me. Do you understand?"

"I am not to change your face from the outside, but I am to change it from the inside," the genie said.

"Exactly so," said Aladdin. "Can you do that?"

"Yes, Master," the genie said, then vanished.

A few minutes later, Aladdin's mother walked through the door in the most sumptuous, queenly robes, with a look of great surprise on her face. "How did I get like this?" she said. Then, looking at Aladdin, she burst into tears. "How beautiful you look, my dear! You must be very happy about your marriage. I have never seen such joy and peace on anyone's face before. I can't look at you without crying for joy."

"Yes," Aladdin said, "I *am* very happy."

They rode to the palace. Aladdin's mother was accompanied by the six slave girls, and Aladdin had twenty slaves preceding him and twenty slaves following him. A great crowd formed on either side of the street. Ten of the slaves were carrying purses of a thousand coins each, and as they walked, they threw the coins into the air to the right and to the left among the people.

Some people in the crowd were speechless with astonishment, but most of the crowd went wild. Many laughed and yelled as they scrambled for the gold that was falling like rain from the sky. Many shouted out their admiration, praise, and blessings to Aladdin, for his generosity, his magnificence, and his great beauty. People knew that his father had been a poor tailor, but there were very few in the crowd who were envious. Almost everyone was happy for him and thought that he deserved his good fortune.

The king was impressed by Aladdin beyond all limits, and Princess Laila fell in love with him at first sight. Her only disappointment was that he wouldn't marry her right away. "There is one thing that I have to do first, Your Majesty," he said to the king. "I want to build the princess a palace as beautiful as she is.

Nothing could be as beautiful as she is, of course, but what I mean is that I want to build her the most beautiful palace in the world, just as she is the most beautiful woman in the world." The princess's heart sank as Aladdin said this. It would take years to build such a palace, she thought, and she longed to hold him in her arms that very night. But being a modest young lady, she said nothing.

"The best place would be on the land facing *my* palace," the king said. "I would like it if my daughter lived that close to me."

"Thank you, Your Majesty," Aladdin said. "That sounds like a very good idea."

Aladdin stayed until midnight, so elaborate and enjoyable were the festivities that the king had prepared for him. When he and his mother returned home, he asked her to wait outside for a few minutes. "There's a little something I have to do," he said.

"All right," said Aladdin's mother. "But make sure that that monster is gone before I come back in."

Aladdin got the lamp from his room and rubbed it. All at once, there was a flash of light, a sound like the flowing of water, and there before his eyes stood the genie of the lamp, in his vest of royal-blue velvet and his royal-blue silk pants. "O Master," the genie said, "your wish is my command. Ask me for anything your heart desires, and I shall make it happen. For I am the slave of whoever owns the blessed lamp."

"I have another job for you," Aladdin said. "Build me, opposite the king's palace, the most magnificent palace in the world. Don't spare yourself, and don't hold anything back. I want my palace to be as much finer than the king's palace as the king's palace is finer than this little cottage."

"Yes, Master," the genie said, then vanished.

Before daybreak the genie returned to Aladdin and said, "Master, the palace is completed. Would you like to see it?"

Aladdin nodded. A split second later he was standing in front of his new palace. The palace was made of the most gorgeous materials: jasper, porphyry, agate, carnelian, alabaster, lapis lazuli, and marble. At the top was a large hall with a dome; each of its four walls contained six windows, and each window had a shutter encrusted with huge diamonds, pearls, emeralds, sapphires, and rubies. The palace's hundred rooms were filled with furniture of the rarest and most elegant woods and fabrics, crafted by master carpenters and artisans, and the walls were hung with paintings surpassing the greatest masterpieces of the ages. The treasury, a cavernous room in the basement, was piled from floor to ceiling with sacks of gold, silver, and precious stones. Next to it, in a storeroom, there was row upon row of chests packed with precious garments and cloth, the finest velvets, silks, and gold-lined brocades from China, India, and the lands of the Arabs. The stables contained two hundred horses, all of which were as splendid as the stallion that the genie had brought Aladdin before, with riders, grooms, huntsmen, hunting equipment, and jewel-studded saddles and bridles. On the first floor, there was a suite of rooms for Aladdin's mother. There was a whole floor of offices, maintained by a hundred clerks, accountants, lawyers, and military officers. In the kitchen six dozen chefs, cooks, waiters, and wine stewards bowed to Aladdin, surrounded by cooking utensils of silver and gold. All through the palace, hundreds of beautiful, sumptuously dressed slaves and slave girls stood at attention, ready to do their master's bidding. There were a hundred particularly lovely slave girls whose only job was to wait on the princess.

Aladdin was deeply moved by the splendor of his palace.

Magnificent is too poor a word for this, he thought.

"I hope that I have done everything to your satisfaction, Master," said the genie.

"Yes, genie," Aladdin said, "and far more than that. You have done a job excellent beyond my imagining."

"You are very kind, Master," the genie said.

"There's just one thing that I forgot to ask for," Aladdin said. "I want you to bring me a carpet made of the finest gold-woven brocade, and I want it to be so long that the princess can walk on it from the front gate of her father's palace to the front gate of my palace—I mean, *our* palace."

"Done!" said the genie.

When the king woke up and saw Aladdin's palace from his bedroom window, he could hardly believe his eyes; he had to rub them to make sure that he wasn't dreaming. The first thing he did was wake up the princess. She was just as amazed. She was also overjoyed. *How wonderful!* she thought. *This means that we won't have to wait to be married.*

And married they were, that very day. The palaces, the city hall, and all the principal buildings were decorated for the occasion. You could hear music and singing everywhere. Crowds

filled the streets, and Aladdin's slaves walked among them scattering gold coins. The people were delirious with joy.

After the wedding, Aladdin and Princess Laila walked on the beautiful, flowered rug from the front gate of the king's palace to the front gate of their own palace. When they got to their bedroom, they said good night to all the beautiful young men and women who were waiting on them, and they closed the door behind them. It was the first time they had ever been alone together. They turned to each other, and it felt as if they had always been standing there, gazing into each other's eyes.

Three years went by. Aladdin and the princess were very happy together. Their love grew and deepened every day.

Whenever Aladdin left the palace, he took along two slaves whose job was to scatter gold coins among the people. He didn't do this to be popular, but because he remembered growing up poor and wanted to share his good fortune with everyone. Every Friday he would open the doors to his treasury, and his bankers and accountants, with their secretaries, would stand outside it and distribute money and food to the needy. His chief physicians and nurses would also be there, offering free medical care to the sick.

There was not a single person in the city who didn't praise Aladdin for his great kindness and generosity. He was more beloved than the king himself. Even his rivals for power gave him full credit. "He is a man of perfect integrity," they would say. "We don't know how he acquired his wealth, but he uses it in the best possible way."

In addition to all his other fine qualities, Aladdin showed remarkable courage in a war that broke out during the second year of his marriage. Enemies of the king crossed the border and attacked several villages, burning and killing as they went. The king appointed Aladdin commander in chief, and he marched to the border at the head of the king's forces. When the two armies met, Aladdin charged through the enemy's lines with drawn sword and put them to flight. The victory was complete. Aladdin returned to the city with only a slight wound on his shoulder. There was a huge celebration. And everyone—from the king, the nobles, and the common people to Aladdin's own employees and slaves—loved and respected him more than ever.

CHAPTER 13

Meanwhile, in Morocco, the sorcerer had an uneasy feeling. "It has been fifteen years now since that wretched little guttersnipe Aladdin died trying to steal my lamp. It must be time now to go back and get it." He did a long, complicated magic ritual, and at the end he looked into the center stone of his crystal necklace. But instead of seeing an image of the lamp, as he expected, what he saw was Aladdin's face, grown-up, handsome, and radiant with joy.

"Curses!" said the sorcerer. "Somehow he must have escaped. And I'll bet he's been taking advantage of my lamp, the little good-for-nothing. If it hadn't been for me, he'd be a beggar. And he's probably a rich man by now, if he hasn't frittered away his power by asking for foolish things. I'd better return to China, kill him, and reclaim my lamp and my ring."

It took the sorcerer a long time to travel all the way from Morocco, across North Africa, Arabia, Persia, across the great desert, across the vast distances of the empire of China, to the city where Aladdin lived. When he finally arrived, he checked in at an inn and rested for the night.

The next morning he went to the most popular teahouse in the city to gather news. Everyone was talking about Aladdin, about his achievements and his wonderful marriage and his splendid palace. The sorcerer turned to the man sitting at the nearest table and said, "Sir, I couldn't help overhearing your conversation. Who is this you're talking about?"

"You must be a stranger," said the man. "Everyone in China knows about Prince Aladdin. I thought that everyone in the whole world knew about him."

"I have come from very far away," the sorcerer said.

"From the moon?" the man said. The other men sitting at his table laughed.

"Forgive my ignorance," said the sorcerer. "I am eager to hear more about this great prince."

After listening to the men talk about Aladdin's accomplishments for the next hour, the sorcerer said to one of them, "Can you take me to the prince's famous palace? I would love to see it."

"Of course," the man said, and immediately he led the sorcerer there.

The sorcerer was furious. "All this could have been mine," he said to himself as he stared at Aladdin's palace. Angry, envious thoughts crawled all over his mind like ants over a half-eaten apple.

Back at the inn the sorcerer asked the innkeeper about

Aladdin. “He is said to be the most remarkable man in China,” the sorcerer said. “I would love to get a glimpse of him, even from a distance.”

“Oh, that’s not difficult, sir,” the innkeeper said. “He is not at all standoffish, like some of the nobility, who think they’re too good for common folks like us. You can usually see him walking around town several days a week, when he isn’t engaged in state business or sitting in the palace gardens with Princess Laila. They spend a lot of time together, you know, reading poetry or listening to music. They have a whole staff of poets and musicians.”

“Well,” the sorcerer said, “I suppose today is as good a day as any.”

“As a matter of fact, sir, it isn’t,” said the innkeeper. “The prince happens to be away on a state mission. People say that he’ll be back in about a week.”

That’s all I need to know, the sorcerer thought.

Without losing a moment, he went to a coppersmith’s shop and bought three dozen brand-new lamps. He put them in a large basket and walked to the open square in front of Aladdin’s palace. Then he began shouting, “Old lamps for new! Who will exchange old lamps for new? All you good women, come and see! Old lamps for new!”

Soon there was a crowd of people around him. They all thought that he was crazy. Who in his right mind would trade brand-new lamps for old ones? “The poor man must not know what he’s doing,” they said. Most of them pitied him and didn’t want to take advantage of his insanity. But a few of the poorer

women went to their kitchens and brought back their battered old lamps. The sorcerer cheerfully gave them shiny new ones from his basket.

"What is all that commotion?" Princess Laila said to one of her slave girls. They were watching from one of the windows in the palace dome.

"I don't know, Your Highness," the slave girl said. "Would you like me to find out?"

"Please," said the princess.

When the slave girl came back, she said, "It's an old man, Your Highness, with a basket of lamps. He's shouting, 'Old lamps for new! Who will exchange old lamps for new?' People are saying he's out of his mind."

"Really?" said the princess. "Poor old man. Why do you think he's trading his new lamps for old ones?"

"Who knows, Your Highness?" the slave girl said. "Crazy people have crazy ideas."

"But maybe he really has a use for those old lamps," the princess said. "Do we have any around?"

"Yes, Your Highness," the slave girl said, "as a matter of fact, we do. There's an old lamp in the back of one of the closets in Prince Aladdin's chambers. I noticed it several weeks ago."

Aladdin had told Princess Laila about everything else in his life, but he had never mentioned the lamp to her. "Well," she said, "just to make the old man happy, give that lamp to him, and give him this also." She handed the slave girl a purse containing five gold coins.

A short time later the slave girl returned. "He really is insane, Your Highness. When I gave him the old lamp, he laughed like a hyena and started kissing it all over. Then he stuck it in his breast pocket. I tried to give him your purse, but he wouldn't take any notice of me. His mind was obviously somewhere else. He dropped the basket of new lamps and just walked away. I called to him, but he wouldn't stop."

The sorcerer was delirious with joy. He walked as fast as he could to the city gates and into the wilderness. When he was sure that nobody could see him, he took out the lamp and rubbed it.

All at once there was a flash of light, a sound like the crashing of thunder, and there before his eyes stood the genie of the lamp, in a vest of black velvet and black silk pants. "O Master," the genie said, "your wish is my command. Ask me for anything your heart desires, and I shall make it happen. For I am the slave of whoever owns the blessed lamp."

"Slave, pick up Aladdin's palace and everyone in it," said the sorcerer, "and carry it to my home in Morocco. And when you're finished, carry me there, too."

"Yes, Master," the genie said. A small tear trickled from his right eye.

CHAPTER 14

The next morning the king looked out his bedroom window, as he did every morning after he got out of bed, because it warmed his heart to see the splendid palace where his beloved daughter lived. But this morning when he looked out the window, there was no palace. The ground was level. There was nothing there.

The king could hardly believe his eyes; he had to rub them to make sure that he wasn't dreaming. When he looked again, there was still nothing. How could this be? How could a whole palace suddenly disappear and not leave a trace behind?

Quickly the king's astonishment turned to grief and rage. Where was Princess Laila? Gone, along with the rest of Aladdin's palace. It was all Aladdin's fault. It *had* to be. Who else was responsible for building the palace overnight? Who else could be responsible for making it vanish into thin air?

By now the king was shaking with fury. "Summon the prime minister!" he shouted to the slave nearest him.

The prime minister arrived within minutes. "Where is Aladdin?" the king shouted.

"Don't you remember, Your Majesty?" the prime minister said. "You sent him on a diplomatic mission. He'll be back in a few days."

"Don't you dare question my memory!" the king bellowed. "I don't care where Aladdin is, or who remembers it! I want him brought back immediately, and I want him brought back in chains!"

"Yes, Your Majesty," said the prime minister, with an inward smile. (He had always thought that Aladdin was a commoner and an upstart.)

Two days later, Aladdin was brought back to the city by a troop of soldiers, his hands and feet bound in chains. When people saw that he had been taken prisoner, they realized that the king intended to kill him. And since they loved Aladdin so much, they took their weapons, swarmed out of their houses, and hurried after the soldiers to see how they could help.

The soldiers reached the palace and brought Aladdin to the executioner's stand. The executioner tied a blindfold around Aladdin's eyes, pushed his head onto the chopping block, walked around him three times, and stood beside him, with his ax upraised.

By now the crowd had broken through the palace gates and surrounded the palace. Thousands of people were waving their weapons in the air and shouting, "Let Aladdin go! If you hurt him, we will destroy the palace and everyone in it! Let Aladdin go, right now!"

The king and the prime minister were watching from the

window. "You've stirred up a hornets' nest, Your Majesty," the prime minister said. "These people mean business. If Aladdin is executed, they'll storm the palace, and that will be the end of you and of me. I think it would be a good idea to pardon him—the sooner the better."

The king was sweating with fear. He signaled to the executioner to stop the proceedings, then sent a herald out to announce to the crowd that Aladdin had been pardoned. When the crowd heard the news, they began to cheer. Soon they dispersed and went back to their homes peacefully.

The herald brought Aladdin to the king's chambers. When Aladdin entered the room, he bowed deeply to the king and said, "Your Majesty, you've been so kind to me. You've been like a father, and much more than a father. Tell me, please, what I have done to cause your displeasure?"

"Traitor!" the king shouted. "How dare you play the innocent! Are you pretending not to know what's happened?"

"I swear to you, Your Majesty," Aladdin said. "I have no idea what you're talking about."

"Look out this window, then, you miserable wretch," the king shouted, "and tell me what you see!"

Aladdin was astonished to see no sign of his glorious palace. The ground where it had stood was absolutely bare.

"I don't know what to say, Your Majesty," Aladdin said. "I don't know what could have happened."

"And where is my daughter?" the king said, bursting into tears. "Where is my beloved daughter? What have you done with her?"

"I assure you, Your Majesty," Aladdin said, "that I don't

know where she can be. This is certainly not my doing. I love the princess more than life itself. I would die before I would let her be harmed. You must know that by now."

"Then find her and bring her back," the king sobbed. "My heart is breaking. If you don't bring her back, I'll die. But before I die, I swear to you that I'll cut off your head."

"I will find her, Your Majesty," Aladdin said. "But grant me forty days. If I don't bring her back to you within forty days, you can go ahead and kill me."

"That's a deal," said the king. "If you don't find her, I will die of a broken heart, and you will die of a severed head."

Bewildered and distraught, Aladdin wandered through the streets of the city. He didn't know what to do. He didn't have the slightest idea how to begin his search for the princess. (He was so grief-stricken that he completely forgot about the sorcerer's ring, which was still on the middle finger of his left hand.) He asked a few of his friends and acquaintances if they knew where the palace had gone, but they looked at him as if he'd gone insane.

Thirty-nine days went by. Aladdin wandered through the whole city and the surrounding countryside. He slept very little during this time and ate only to keep up his strength. Finally one evening, in despair, he wandered to the banks of a river and, for an instant, thought of drowning himself. When he realized what he was about to do, he put his palms together and began to pray. "Dear God," he said, "please help me. Please let me find my beloved and—"

As he said these last words, his right hand happened to make a tiny movement, so that his fingers, ever so gently, rubbed against the ring. All at once there was a flash of light, a sound like the crying of a puppy, and there before his eyes stood the genie of the ring, in his vest of crimson velvet and his royal-blue silk pants. "O Master, your wish is my command," the genie said. "Ask me for anything your heart desires, and I shall make it happen. For I am the slave of whoever wears the blessed ring."

"Oh, thank God!" Aladdin said. "You can't know how happy I am to see you, genie."

The genie bowed.

"Here's what I need," Aladdin said, "I need you to bring back my wife and my palace and everything inside it. Please do this right away. I can't wait a moment longer."

"I am sorry, Master," the genie said, "but I cannot. I should have said, 'Ask for *almost* anything your heart desires.' This is the one exception. Only the slave of the lamp can perform this task. It is a task that is forbidden to me."

"If you can't bring the princess to me," Aladdin said, "can you take me to the princess?"

"Yes, Master," the genie said. "I shall transport you to Morocco as soon as you give me the command."

"To Morocco?" Aladdin said. "Of course! The sorcerer is the one who's behind all this! I should have known. Take me to my palace, right away."

"Done!" said the genie.

Instantly Aladdin found himself standing in front of his palace. The landscape was entirely different—palm trees, the

air dry and warm, camels grazing—but the palace looked exactly the same. "Now bind the sorcerer," Aladdin said, "and bring him to me."

"I cannot do that, either," said the genie. "I am terribly sorry, Master. But the sorcerer keeps the lamp in his breast pocket at all times. And since the slave of the lamp is more powerful than I, I cannot fulfill any command that concerns the owner of the lamp. Ask for whatever else you desire, and I shall be happy to obey you."

"Bring me the princess, then," Aladdin said.

"O Master," the genie said, "I am sorry to disappoint you again, but the princess is in the sorcerer's power, and I am forbidden to interfere. You will have to rescue her yourself."

"But how can I do that?" said Aladdin. "What do you suggest?"

"My job, Master, is not to suggest, but to obey," the genie said, and he vanished.

Aladdin felt very tired and confused. He lay down under a palm tree at the foot of the wall around the palace. *At least I know where the princess is,* he thought. *I'll sleep a little, and things will be clearer when I wake up.*

Early the next morning, when Princess Laila's favorite slave girl opened the shutters in the princess's bedroom, she saw Aladdin lying under the tree. "Your Highness, Your Highness!" she cried out. "It's Prince Aladdin! He's come to save us!"

The princess hurried to the window. Just as she looked out, Aladdin awoke. When they saw each other, their hearts filled with joy.

Aladdin ran to the palace and stopped just under the princess's window. He was about to shout to her, but the princess put her index finger over her lips, then pointed down to the secret door to her chambers. A few moments later a slave girl opened the door, and Aladdin walked in.

Princess Laila and Aladdin embraced. They covered each other's cheeks with kisses. They wanted to know everything that had happened to the other during the last thirty-nine days, but there was only time for a few sentences. "How are you?" "I love you so much." "I missed you."

Aladdin had to think fast since, for all he knew, the sorcerer might walk in at any moment. "Tell me one thing," he said to the princess. "How has he been treating you? Has he been horrible?"

"No, not horrible," said the princess. "Just pathetic. He wants to marry me. He keeps saying that you've been executed and that I must forget you. I never believed him, of course."

"Of course," Aladdin said.

"But how did all this happen?" the princess asked.

"Somehow he got control of my lamp," Aladdin said.

"Do you mean the old lamp in the back of your closet?" the princess said. "I gave that to a madman who was trading old lamps for new."

"That madman was him," said Aladdin. "There's a genie in that lamp. That's how you and the whole palace were transported here to Morocco."

"Oh, dear," the princess said, bursting into tears. "Then it was all my fault."

"My poor darling," Aladdin said. "It was no one's fault. You didn't know. If it was anyone's fault, it was mine, because I didn't tell you about the lamp and didn't keep it safe enough. But all that is in the past. The question is, What can we do now?"

"Well," the princess said, "the old man *says* he's in love with me. He really tries to treat me very nicely."

"And . . ." Aladdin said.

"And I was just thinking that maybe I could invite him to dinner."

"And . . ."

"And pour some wine for him. I know he likes wine. I've seen him drink it."

"I'm not following you. So you pour some wine. What good will that do?"

"Well, sweetheart," said the princess, "if you could somehow find a powerful drug that will put him to sleep—"

"You'll put it in his wine?"

"Yes, and when he's unconscious—"

"Yes, yes! When he's unconscious, we can take the lamp out of his breast pocket, and he won't have any power over us!"

"But how will you find the drug?" the princess asked. "You don't know the language here. How will you ask for it?"

"Hmm," said Aladdin. He thought for a moment. "I know the way," he said. "You wouldn't mind if I summoned a genie, would you, sweetheart?"

"Of course not," the princess said. "Why would I mind?"

"Well," Aladdin said, "some women are a little . . . let's say, timid."

"You're thinking of your mother," the princess said, smiling. "You know I'm not like that. You shouldn't even have to ask."

"I just wanted to make sure," Aladdin said.

"You're going to ask the genie for the drug?" the princess asked.

"I can't do that," Aladdin said. "The genie isn't able to fulfill any command that concerns the owner of the lamp. But I have another idea."

He rubbed the ring. All at once there was a flash of light, a sound like the beating of rain against a window, and there before their eyes stood the genie of the ring, in his vest of crimson velvet and his royal-blue silk pants. "O Master, your wish is my command," the genie said. "Ask me for anything—*almost* anything—your heart desires, and I shall make it happen. For I am the slave of whoever wears the blessed ring."

"Genie," said Aladdin, "do you know the Moroccan language?"

"Yes, Master," the genie said. "I know all human languages."

"Then tell me how you say in Moroccan, 'I want to buy your strongest sleep-producing drug. I want a drug that will make a man fall asleep in an instant.' "

The genie told him how to say that.

"Now I'll go buy the drug," Aladdin said to the princess, "and you can invite the old man to dinner as soon as you see him. I'll wait outside your window. Give me a sign, and I'll come up."

Three hours later Aladdin returned from the bazaar, where he had found a dealer in medicines and drugs. The princess was waiting at the window. She motioned Aladdin toward the secret door.

"I found it!" Aladdin said when he had entered. He handed her the drug. "Just dissolve this powder in his wine, and he'll fall asleep."

"Easier said than done," the princess said. "What if he notices the powder?"

"I know you'll find a way," said Aladdin. "Now, hide me in your closet. As soon as the old man is unconscious, call me, and I'll come out."

"All right," the princess said. They looked at each other for a few moments. "Are you nervous?"

"A little," Aladdin said.

"So am I."

At seven o'clock the sorcerer arrived at the princess's chambers.

"Come in, come in," the princess said. "My ladies have prepared a sumptuous meal for us. Sit down. Have a glass of wine."

"Thank you, my dear," the sorcerer said, taking a seat at the dinner table. "I'm so glad that you're feeling better. Tears never did anyone any good."

"I have cried an ocean of tears," the princess said, pouring him a glass of red wine. "Now it's time to stop mourning."

"Yes," the sorcerer said, drinking the wine. "Your husband is dead and gone. Why should you spend your life mourning him? You are young and beautiful. You have your life ahead of you."

"I'm sure you're right," said the princess. "Life is full of the most wonderful surprises. Who knows what lies ahead? Have some more wine." And she poured more wine into his glass.

"Once you have forgotten Aladdin," the sorcerer said, "you'll find it easy to love me."

"You could be right," the princess said.

"When you get to know me better, you'll see that I'm a very lovable man," the sorcerer said. "I'm a very *wealthy* man, and the wealthier a man is, the more lovable he is. "Don't you agree?"

"I never thought of it that way," the princess said. "But have some more wine. Dinner will be coming soon." And she poured more wine into his glass.

"Yes," said the sorcerer, "I can give you everything your little heart desires: diamonds, pearls, emeralds, rubies, whatever you want. Just name it, and I will make it happen. I have my ways. In my country they call me the greatest sorcerer in the world."

"Really?" said the princess. "That's quite a distinction."

"Yes," the sorcerer said, "and they arc right. Thc greatest sorcerer in the world, that's what I am. I can't say that I am the *happiest* man in the world. But if you marry me, I will be. The happiest man in the world, I mean. I will be the happiest man in the world if you marry me."

By now the sorcerer was getting drunk. He was slurring his words and rocking back and forth in his chair.

"I hear you," said the princess. "But I need time. Surely you can understand that. All this is so sudden. It takes time for feelings to change. Have another glass of wine." And she poured more wine into his glass.

"I don't mind if I do," the sorcerer said, and he drank the wine in one gulp. "Very good wine, too. What was I saying? Ah, yes! Of course it takes time, but time is precisely what we have.

We have plenty of time. That is, we have as much of it as we need. I am not a man in a hurry. I am not a man in a rush. I am not an unreasonable man. I am not a man with a full glass."

"Then let me pour you some more," the princess said.

"Thank you, my dear," said the sorcerer, and again he drank the wine in one gulp. "But will you excuse me for a moment? I've drunk so much that I have to go to the bathroom now."

"Of course," the princess said.

After the sorcerer had wobbled out of the room, Princess Laila took out the powder, poured another glass of wine, then mixed the powder into it.

Soon the sorcerer returned and sat down at the table. "Now then, my dear—now then, now then," he said, "what were we talking about?"

"I was about to tell you," the princess said, "that in my country we have a custom. At the beginning of dinner, the host exchanges glasses with the guest, and both drink to each other's health."

"A fine custom," said the sorcerer. "An excellent custom. I love that custom. Let's drink to that custom."

"Then hand me your glass," the princess said. "And I'll hand you mine."

"Steady, steady," the sorcerer said to himself. His hand was shaking.

"Now let's drink," the princess said.

No sooner had the sorcerer taken a drink from this glass than he fell over onto the rug and lay there completely motionless.

"Aladdin!" the princess called. "It's done!"

Aladdin stepped out of the closet, walked over to the sorcerer, reached into his breast pocket, and took out the magic lamp. "It's done, sweetheart," he said. "We're free now."

"But what should we do about the old man?" the princess said.

"I suppose I could kill him," Aladdin said. "But that doesn't feel right."

"Not to me, either," the princess said. "He hasn't really done you any harm. He *tried* to hurt you, but he didn't succeed."

"Actually," Aladdin said, "he hasn't hurt anyone but himself. His whole life has been about finding a treasure that wasn't even his to begin with. He has just made himself miserable with envy and disappointment. I feel sorry for him."

"So do I," said the princess.

"And to tell the truth," Aladdin said, "I'm very grateful to him. If it hadn't been for him, I wouldn't have become the person I am, and I would never have been able to marry you."

"Yes," the princess said. "In a very strange way, we both owe him a lot."

"Still, we can't just let him go," Aladdin said. "He's a dangerous man. I suppose I could command the genie of the lamp to imprison him somewhere. I could seal him up in a cave forever. Or I could have him carried off to a tribe of savages a thousand miles away."

"True," said the princess. "But that doesn't seem very kind. Besides, he is such a clever man that he might escape."

"You're right," Aladdin said. "Hmm."

They were both silent for a while. Then the princess's face lit up. "I've got it!" she said. "Summon the genie of the lamp."

"Good," said Aladdin, and he rubbed the lamp. All at once there was a flash of light, a sound like the faintest whisper, and there before their eyes stood the genie of the lamp, in his vest of royal-blue velvet and his royal-blue silk pants. "O Master," the genie said, "your wish is my command. Ask me for anything your heart desires, and I shall make it happen. For I am the slave of whoever owns the blessed lamp."

"Genie," Aladdin said, "my wife has a command for you. Is that all right? Can she command you, even though I am the owner of the lamp?"

"Yes, Master," said the genie. "Husband and wife are one flesh. Her wish is my command."

"Well then, genie," the princess said. "I command you to erase all memory of us from the old man's mind. Erase all memory of the lamp, of the treasure, and of you. And erase all memory of sorcery and magic. When he wakes up, let him be just a simple man, with a simple past that never happened."

"Yes, Mistress," the genie said. "It is already done."

"Brilliant!" said Aladdin. "This way we don't have to hurt him, and he can no longer hurt us. Why didn't *I* think of that?"

"I'm sure you would have," the princess said, raising an eyebrow, "if only we had waited one more second."

Aladdin smiled. Then he said to the genie, "Take us home now, and put this palace exactly where it was before."

"As you wish, Master," said the genie. "I am glad that you have the lamp again."

CHAPTER 17

The next morning was the fortieth day, the day of Aladdin's deadline. The king woke up as usual, and as usual he walked, slowly and sadly, to his bedroom window. He looked out, expecting to see the level ground that meant that his daughter was still missing. But to his amazement, there before him was Aladdin's palace, in all its splendor. He could hardly believe his eyes; he had to rub them to make sure that he wasn't dreaming.

Soon his bedroom door opened, and Princess Laila walked in, with Aladdin right behind her. The princess ran into her father's arms, and they embraced. They were so overcome with emotion that they didn't know whether they were laughing or crying.

It was a long time before they could speak. Finally the princess told her father the whole story, how she had given away the magic lamp, how the sorcerer had transported the whole palace to Morocco, how Aladdin had rescued her, and how the sorcerer was now a harmless old man who had gone into the used-lamp business.

After she had finished, the king turned to Aladdin and said, "I have a request."

"Ask me anything, Your Majesty," Aladdin said. "I will be happy to oblige."

"My request," the king said, "is that you forgive me for my thoughtlessness. I almost took your life, because I leapt to the wrong conclusion. It was very stupid of me. I was so upset about my daughter that I just couldn't think straight. Please forgive me."

"Of course I do," said Aladdin. "You thought I had harmed your daughter. It's hard to be fair when that's what you believe. But it all turned out well in the end."

"Yes, it did," the king said. "And now that I have you both back safe and sound, I will try to be wiser in the future."

The king kept his word, and from that day on, he was a much more sensible person. He even fired his prime minister and appointed Aladdin in his place.

After a dozen years he died, and since the princess was his only child, Aladdin became king. He treated his people with so much justice and wisdom that they began to call him King Aladdin the Kind. Everyone loved him, and everyone delighted in the love that he and Queen Laila had for each other and for their children. They lived a long life together, filled with happiness and charity and peace.

AFTERWORD

The collection of anonymous tales known in English as *The Thousand and One Nights* or *The Arabian Nights* is universally considered to be among the classics of world literature. The tales originated from the Indian, Persian, Arab, and Chinese merchants who traveled on the Silk Road between northern China and the Middle East. These travelers would stop in caravanserais for the night and relax by telling stories.

The tales circulated orally for hundreds of years and were kept alive by professional storytellers, who would recite them in bazaars and coffee houses in Persia and throughout the Arab world. The first written version that we know of is a book of Persian tales called *Hazar Afsana* (*A Thousand Tales*), which was translated into Arabic during the ninth century; in 947, the Arab historian al-Mas'udi refers to this book as *Alf Layla* (*A Thousand Nights*). Neither the Persian nor the Arabic book has survived.

Except for a single-page fragment from the ninth century, the oldest surviving text is a three-volume Syrian manuscript that dates from the fourteenth century. This collection contains only 282 of the 1001 nights. *Thousand and one* was originally a symbolic phrase meaning "a very large number." Later, literal-minded copyists kept adding tales from the Indian, Persian, and Turkish traditions, so that the total would add up to exactly a thousand and one tales.

The four earliest printed editions are known as Calcutta I (1814–18), Breslau (1825–43), Bulaq (1835), and Calcutta II (1839–42). The origins of these texts are unclear. Scholars consider the Bulaq text to be the most significant.

The first European translation of the *Nights* was by Antoine Galland (1646–1715). His twelve-volume version (first edition, 1704) was widely read and had a powerful effect on European literature. The three best-known English translations are by Edward Lane (1839–41), John Payne (1882–84), and Sir Richard Francis Burton (1885–88). T. E. Lawrence ("Lawrence of Arabia") accurately said of them, "The rivalry in English isn't high. Lane is pompous, Payne crabbed, and Burton unreadable."

Galland worked from the fourteenth-century Syrian manuscript, but his translation included a number of tales that he had heard in 1709 from his friend Hanna Diab, a Maronite Christian from Aleppo. These additional tales include "Aladdin" and "Ali Baba." None of them have been found in any surviving Arabic manuscript predating Galland, and scholars think that subsequent Arabic versions are actually retranslations from Galland's French version. This doesn't necessarily mean that "Aladdin" and "Ali Baba" are not very old stories; we simply don't have the manuscript evidence.

I chose "Aladdin" and "Ali Baba" for this book because they are probably the most famous tales in *The Thousand and One Nights*. "Abu Keer and Abu Seer," which is much less well known, is the most modern of all the tales. It can be dated because of its reference to tobacco, which was introduced to Europe from the Americas by 1560 and didn't become common in the Near East until the seventeenth century.

For "Ali Baba" and "Aladdin," my starting point was the translations of Lane, Burton, and Husain Haddawy (1995); for "Abu Keer and Abu Seer," I used the Burton translation, which is the only one of the three that includes it. My retellings are free adaptations. I have kept the main story lines, but I have abridged, deleted, and expanded incidents, added and deleted dialogue, modified motivation and character, and made whatever other changes seemed appropriate in order to bring these tales to life in the English of today.